Dear Reader,

The book you've just bought from my "Second Chances" series is truly evidence of the second chances God gives us. The books in this series have been published before, some by Dell, some by Harlequin, others by Silhouette and HarperCollins. I was a Christian when I entered the romance market in 1983, hoping to take the world by storm. What I found, instead, was that the world took me by storm. One compromise led to another, until my books did not read like books written by a Christian. Not only were they not pleasing to God, but they embraced a worldview that opposed Christ's teachings. In the interest of being successful, I had compartmentalized my faith. I trusted Christ for my salvation, but not much else. Like the Prodigal Son, I had taken my inheritance and left home to do things my own way.

I love that parable because it so reflects my life. My favorite part is when Jesus said, "But while he was still a long way off, his father saw him . . ." I can picture that father scanning the horizon every day, hoping for his son's return. God did that for me. While I was still a long way off, God saw me coming. Early in 1994, when I yearned to be closer to God and realized that my writing was a wall between us, that my way had not been the best way, I promised God that I would never write anything again that did not glorify him. At that moment, it was as if God came running out to meet me. I gave up my secular career and began to write Christian books.

Shortly after I signed a contract for Zondervan to publish my suspense series, "The Sun Coast Chronicles," something extraordinary happened. The rights to some of my earlier romance novels were given back to me, and I was free to do whatever I wanted with them. At first, I thought of shelving them, but then, in God's gentle way, he reminded me that I was free to rewrite them, and this time, get them right. So I set about to rewrite these stories the way God originally intended them.

As you read these stories, keep in mind that they're not just about second chances, they are second chances. I hope you enjoy them.

In Christ,
Terri Blackstock

Books by Terri Blackstock

Soul Restoration
Emerald Windows

Restoration Series

1 | *Last Light*
2 | *Night Light*

Cape Refuge Series

1 | *Cape Refuge*
2 | *Southern Storm*
3 | *River's Edge*
4 | *Breaker's Reef*

Newpointe 911

1 | *Private Justice*
2 | *Shadow of Doubt*
3 | *Word of Honor*
4 | *Trial by Fire*
5 | *Line of Duty*

Sun Coast Chronicles

1 | *Evidence of Mercy*
2 | *Justifiable Means*
3 | *Ulterior Motives*
4 | *Presumption of Guilt*

Second Chances

1 | *Never Again Good-bye*
2 | *When Dreams Cross*
3 | *Blind Trust*
4 | *Broken Wings*

With Beverly LaHaye

1 | *Seasons Under Heaven*
2 | *Showers in Season*
3 | *Times and Seasons*
4 | *Season of Blessing*

Novellas

Seaside

SECOND S2C CHANCES

WHEN DREAMS CROSS

TERRI BLACKSTOCK

ZONDERVAN®

GRAND RAPIDS, MICHIGAN 49530 USA

ZONDERVAN.COM/
AUTHORTRACKER

ZONDERVAN®

When Dreams Cross

Requests for information should be addressed to:

Zondervan, *Grand Rapids, Michigan 49530*

Library of Congress Cataloging-in-Publication Data

Blackstock, Terri, 1957–.
When dreams cross / Terri Blackstock.
p. cm. — (Second chances)
ISBN-10: 0-310-20709-6
ISBN-13: 978-0-310-20709-2
I. Title. II. Series: Blackstock, Terri, 1957– Second chances.
PS3552.L34285W48 1997
813'.54—dc 20 96-35255

Published in association with the literary agency of Alive Communications, Inc., 7680 Goddard Street, Suite 200, Colorado Springs, CO 80920.

Interior design by Amy E. Langeler

Printed in the United States of America

06 07 08 09 10 11 12 • 31 30 29 28 27 26 25 24 23 22 21 20 19 18 17 16

This book is lovingly dedicated to the Nazarene.

Chapter One

The past was a funny thing. It had a way of catching up with you—no matter how fast you ran. Andi Sherman realized now that it was gaining on her.

There was no way around it. The Khaki Kangaroo cartoon was the only one that had the kind of characters she had wanted for her amusement park. But she had resisted choosing it, because she wasn't sure she was up to dealing with the baggage that came with it.

But letting personal feelings influence her business decisions would have disappointed her father, who had trusted her to take over his dream when others saw her as not much more than a kid. She had something to prove now. Even if it meant working with Justin Pierce.

Andi sighed. "It's perfect, Wes. That cartoon is the only one that strikes the right chord."

The builder nodded. "You chose it, Andi. You knew those characters were perfect for Promised Land the first time you saw them. I did, too."

Andi turned around in her leather swivel chair and stared down at some papers on her desk. Of course she had known it was perfect. But that was before she had learned that Justin Pierce was its animator.

Justin Pierce. She had counted on spending the rest of her life without seeing him again.

She raised her eyes to Wes, her old friend and the builder who would incorporate these characters into the rides. As she watched, he rolled a purple Tootsie Pop around in his mouth, one that he'd probably bought for his daughter, Amy. "It doesn't matter, though," she said. "Justin probably won't come anyway. He's already an hour and a half late."

Wes took the sucker from his mouth and surveyed the uncharacteristic tension on Andi's face. "Justin's not stupid. If he has any business sense at all, he'll come."

"If it were just business," Andi said in a hollow voice, "it wouldn't be that hard."

Standing up, she went to the window, hands jammed in the pockets of her slacks. The cool pink blouse she wore provided a soft contrast to the tan on Andi's arms. Absently, her hand went up to tuck a stray strand of hair into the French braid at the nape of her neck. If only she could put this off until another day, she thought.

"Andi," Wes said, his gentle voice cutting into her thoughts to remind her he was still there. "Eight years is a long time, and you were both practically kids. Don't you think he's put all that behind him by now?"

Andi breathed a silent laugh. She had never been able to completely put it behind her. But she had lost more when the relationship ended than he had. She turned back to Wes, who'd been friends with them both when they were all involved in a Christian discipling group in college. "Of course he has. I'm just worried about those resentments he had toward me the last time I saw him. They might get in the way of my offer."

Wes stood up and stuck the Tootsie Pop back in his mouth. "Those resentments were unfounded. And your father was wrong. Everything that happened was wrong."

His words were slurred around the candy, making what he said seem less important, but Andi knew better. "Surely the past won't cloud a business deal like this."

Surely, Andi thought with a sarcastic lift of her brows. But unless Justin Pierce had changed, she knew there would be trouble.

The secretary's warning buzz and the knock on the heavy oak door paralyzed Andi. She glanced at the closed circuit television screen behind her desk—the one that monitored the goings and comings outside her office—and saw the man she'd been waiting for. She looked at Wes, trying not to look as fragile as she felt. He seemed torn between compassion and amusement as he sat on the edge of her desk. "It's him," he said.

"I can't believe he came."

Wes started to the door. "I'll let him in, then leave you two alone."

"No, stay," she said quickly. "We'll talk about old times."

He turned back to her. "Andi, Justin and I have kept in touch. He was in my wedding last year, for heaven's sake. If you still want to talk about old times after you've had this meeting, we'll all have dinner tonight. But don't sweat it. It's just Justin."

Just Justin.

The words didn't go together. It was like saying, "Just napalm." Justin Pierce had never been anything that could be preceded by the word *just*.

She went back to her desk but remained standing. Lifting her chin and hardening her green eyes, she told Wes, "Let him in."

Wes opened the door, and Justin stood there, looking as apprehensive, as defensive as she. Surprised to see his old college roommate, Justin let a slow, reluctant grin break across his face.

"Hey, buddy," Wes said, taking his hand in a friendly shake. "How's it going?"

Justin laughed. "Man, I didn't expect to see you here."

"We haven't talked in a few months. This is one of the reasons I've been so busy. Andi hired me to head up the building going on here," he said.

At the mention of her name, Justin's smile faded, and he faced the woman behind the desk. Her smile was tentative, almost awkward. "Thank you for coming, Justin," she said.

For a moment he just stared at her, his cool scrutiny making her wish she had never swallowed her pride and called him. He had not changed. His black hair, tousled by the April breeze, fell over his forehead and ears, ruffling across the collar of his shirt, but he made no attempt to sweep it back into place. One hand rested in the pocket of worn jeans, and his tweed blazer was caught behind his wrist.

Wes was still grinning. "I gotta go, buddy, but we'll get together later, okay?"

"Sure," Justin said.

Wes glanced back at Andi. "You know where I'll be."

Andi nodded.

The door shut behind Wes, but Justin made no move to come further into the room. "You look good," he said in a detached voice. "The years haven't done any damage." His lids hung low over the clear blue of his eyes, like shields poised for battle.

Andi shrugged, hoping to hide her resentment at his observation. Did he expect her to be a forlorn, shriveled creature who'd begun deteriorating the moment he left? "Eight years isn't that long," she said. "I see you haven't changed much either."

She gestured toward a chair, but Justin remained standing, hands in his pockets, his actions punctuating her words. Neither of them had changed; their pride still covered them both like armor. Knowing it was true, that pride was her greatest fault, didn't help her to deal with it or to repent from it. It had brought her to her knees more than once, full of remorse and good intentions, but now she knew it emanated from her as potently as it did from him.

Andi brought her eyes back to Justin, matching chill for chill, and when she finally broke the eye contact and looked at her desk, he sat down. She wondered how long they might have stood there staring at each other across the desk, neither saying a word, if she hadn't broken the gaze first. The very childishness of all that pride made her angry.

Crossing an ankle over a knee, Justin rested his elbows on the arms of his chair and clasped his hands loosely.

"I'll be honest with you," Andi said, forcing herself to meet his gaze again. "I didn't think you'd come."

"I'll be honest with you," he parried, cocking his head. "I didn't plan to. Not until about an hour ago." His eyes strayed to the television monitors behind her desk and, thankful for something to say that was not so fraught with tension, Andi glanced over her shoulder.

"Those are my monitors. They tape everyone who goes or comes through any of the gates."

"Ah, yes," Justin said with a knowing nod. "The Sherman control."

Andi felt a tight pull in her temples. "I'm running a business."

"Running a business," he repeated. "Twenty-nine years old, and all this is yours."

A spark flickered across Andi's eyes. "All mine," she said through tight lips. "And you can believe that I've paid dearly for it. In fact, I wouldn't be where I am if my father wasn't lying in a hospital bed."

Justin leaned his elbows on his knees and studied the lines of his palms. "Sorry," he said, his eyes suddenly soft, the same softness that once had the power to melt her in a single glance. Now she remembered what she had seen in him all those years ago.

He covered his eyes and slid his hands slowly down his face. "I read about your father's accident and his coma. I didn't mean to bring the subject up like that. It was unfair. Lack of sleep sometimes puts me in a sour mood."

"I know the feeling," Andi answered quietly, some of her tension easing with his apology. Leaning back in her chair, she allowed herself to study the fatigue on his face and the weary slump of his shoulders. "You do look tired."

"I work nights," he explained noncommittally. "At the Mutual Bank Building. I'm a security guard there."

"A security guard?" Her eyebrows shot up and she gazed at him with unveiled disbelief. "You went back to that?"

He nodded, glancing at a pencil holder on her desk as if he rued the fact that he'd mentioned it at all. "It supplements my income. Everything my cartoons net goes to pay my staff."

A frown settled between her brows. "But you're an animator. After you changed your major in college—"

"I told my dad that I could never be what he wanted me to be," Justin finished, as if he'd chanted it to himself a thousand times. "But it's gotten me through some rough spots. I'm glad I had the background."

Andi leaned forward, fingering the contracts on her desk, fighting her urge to take up his cause and argue for his talent. "When do you sleep?"

The personal question laced with concern made him look at her for a long moment, a moment charged with electricity. Her heart began to swell. He was here. The old Justin. The first man she had ever loved.

But, as though he were engaged in some emotional struggle, he quickly shifted in his seat and took on that uncaring look again. The prideful Justin, the one who had been as much her enemy as her friend, shrugged and said, "Ordinarily I'd be sleeping right now."

She fought away the emotions on her own face. "Oh. Sorry." Andi cleared her throat and swiveled to the television set that held the tape of his cartoon, "Khaki's Krewe." She flicked it on, deciding it was time to get down to business before the tension thickened another degree. "Then I won't waste any more of your time. I'll get right to the point." The cartoon came to life, and a smile played across Andi's lips. "I understand this is yours." She turned back to Justin, whose eyes had not left her long enough to view his own creation.

"You understand right."

"It's good. Very good."

"Thanks," he said mildly.

"Wes thinks so, too."

Justin frowned. "What gives with Wes? Last I heard, he was working on the new mall."

"He's still working on it," she said, "but it's almost finished. And I was having trouble coordinating all of my builders—they kept clashing with each other—so I brought Wes in to coordinate them all for me. It was a good move. We both have the same vision for the park. It made a huge difference to have someone else who listens to God making decisions."

"Wes always did have his heart in the right place. But I'm a little surprised that would make any difference to you."

Andi leaned forward, frowning. "What do you mean by that?"

"Just that all those altruistic, spiritual dreams of yours must have flown out the window when you got involved with your father's company. When you were nineteen, you were planning to be a missionary in Africa or somewhere by now."

"And so were you," she said in a hollow voice. "Instead, you're working at the Mutual Bank Building as a security guard."

It was a low blow, but no lower than the one he'd just dealt her.

"My cartoons are an evangelism tool," he said. "They touch lives."

"And so will my park."

For a moment there was a thick silence between them, silence wrought with history and bitterness, silence that spoke volumes about betrayal and loyalty, and that fragile emotion called love.

Struggling to get past that history, Andi leaned on her elbows and clasped her hands under her chin. "As I was saying, Justin, the cartoons are good. And I understand that you haven't been able to sell them to a network or any other lucrative medium."

"So far," the animator conceded, leaning back in his seat and resting his chin on his fingers. "I've come close, but the Christian theme and all the biblical parallels play against them. I'll find a place for them soon enough. I'm a patient man."

"You don't have to be," Andi said. She shifted her gaze to the television screen, where the nearsighted farmer was making his way across a cornfield, his animals running ahead of and around him, protecting him without his knowledge from the traps set by the troll.

It was time to make her move.

Andi turned back to Justin, praying he would see the sense in her offer and not some underlying motive. "I have the answer," she announced. "I'd like to buy the exclusive rights to your cartoon and use the characters in Promised Land."

Contrary to Andi's expectations, there was no change in Justin's expression, in his breathing, or in the steadfast way he studied her over steepled fingertips. There was no indication, in fact, that he'd heard her at all.

"Did you hear me?" she asked finally.

"I heard you. It's just that I'm not surprised, really. When your secretary called, I assumed there would be some such offer."

Andi forced a smile. "Good," she said, not quite certain that she meant it. "Then you've thought about it."

He breathed a mirthless laugh. "Thought about it? I guess you could say that. But it didn't take much thought. I have no intention of handing over the exclusive rights to my cartoons to you or anybody else."

Vexation rippled through Andi's stiff muscles, and she cleared her throat and opened the file on her desk. "Justin, I hope you aren't putting our past problems in the way of something that could help us both. You do realize, don't you, that there'll be a lot of money involved?"

"There's always money involved, Andi. Aren't you the one who taught me that?"

She closed her eyes. Of course they couldn't get past that history, that stuffed baggage they both dragged behind them. Some things just didn't go away.

She took a deep breath and decided to face the problems head-on. "You can't blame me for what happened to us, Justin."

"Then who can I blame?"

She got up and shoved her chair back, then crossed her arms and paced over to the window. "My father lied to me, Justin. He told me he'd offered you fifty thousand dollars to break things off with me and leave town, and he said you took it."

"And you believed him!" The words erupted as if they'd been held in too long. "You *believed* that I would take a bribe from him to end my relationship with you."

"Well, you left," she said, spinning around. "You disappeared for a week, without so much as a word. What was I supposed to think?"

"I was furious at your father," he said. "And yeah, I disappeared, because I was angry and upset and didn't know whether to tell you what your father had done and ruin your image of him. I didn't know if we had a future together, if I could stand the constant pressure from the man who never thought I was good enough for his little girl. I didn't know if I could ever be good enough for you, and I had to think—"

"So of course, I was the bad guy. I shouldn't have accused you, Justin . . ."

"You shouldn't have *doubted* me," he said. "You knew what kind of a man I was. Your money and your family were liabilities to me, Andi, not assets."

"I know that."

"Then when did you come to know the truth?" he asked. "When did you finally stop thinking I had been paid off?"

The question hung in the air for a moment. "I knew it the minute you said it," she whispered. "I knew I had made a mistake. But just thinking you had done it became the end of us." She swallowed, tried to control the wobble in her voice. "And then a few years ago, my father's life changed. He became a Christian, Justin, if you can believe that."

Justin looked up at her, doubtful.

"He confessed everything, and I forgave him. I think he even tried to find you, to ask for your forgiveness. But nobody really knew where you were at the time."

He looked down at the plush carpet beneath his feet, and she couldn't tell from his eyes what was going through his mind.

"When we started looking for an animator, Wes brought in your cartoon and included it with the tapes we were considering. When I saw Khaki's Krewe, I knew it was just what we needed, Justin. I had no idea it was yours. I was doubly surprised to find that you were back here, in Shreveport."

"My mother had a stroke two years ago," he said. "I moved back to help out. My staff agreed to come with me. Mom died, eventually."

"Oh, Justin," she cut in. "I didn't know."

"It's okay," he said. "She's with Dad now. She was really suffering. Anyway, we decided to stay here. I inherited their house, so I set up the studio there. We've been working hard to get our cartoons into the right hands. But I don't think I want to hand them over to you. I'm not that hungry."

Andi swallowed the lump in her throat, and slid her hands into her pockets. With a lift of her chin, she walked around her desk to stand in front of him. Her voice was hoarse when she spoke. "Justin, as a businessman you must realize what Promised Land could do for your characters."

A smirk told her he was enjoying this. "Absolutely. Just as you realize what my characters can do for Promised Land."

She locked eyes with him for a moment, then bit her lip and went to peer out the large plateglass window, seeking a way to put this ruinous enmity between them to rest.

He strode toward her. "As I said, I won't give you exclusive rights. But there are other possibilities," he began in a soft, matter-of-fact monotone. "I might consider working *with* you. My staff and I would have to retain absolute control of our characters, have the last word concerning everything that's done with them, and of course continue producing the cartoons. And we would sell them to anyone else we choose. I'm no fool. Profits made from merchandising—like toys or clothes or movies—would go to me, not to you."

She turned to him, her back against the window that held the view of the amusement park that had been the focus of her plans and dreams for six years now. A moment of silence followed as her emerald eyes cut into him with cool contempt. "I don't do business that way, Justin," she said finally. "When something concerns Promised Land, I like to be in control."

A sarcastic smile tipped one side of his full lips. "Like father, like daughter," he mumbled under his breath. "Manipulative, dictatorial . . ."

Andi swallowed and tried to step back, but the window against her back prevented her. "And I suppose I controlled you?" She held his intimidating gaze, refusing to let him know his devastating effect on her.

"Didn't you?" The muscles hinging his jaw rippled. "I've learned a lot of lessons since I saw you last," he said, his voice a harsh whisper. "Hard ones. And you probably have, too. If anything, we're probably both more stubborn than we were before, and you'd have to be crazy to think either of us could compromise."

"Have you learned any lessons about pride or arrogance, Justin?"

His gaze locked with hers. "Have *you?*"

Andi swallowed and stepped away, putting safer distance between them as she cut out a mirthless laugh that contained more emotion than she'd counted on. "Justin, Wes taped that cartoon at two o'clock in the morning at the tail end of a program that no one in his right mind would watch. And you have the nerve to pretend my offer doesn't mean anything to you? If I were you, I'd be thinking about my future."

"Don't tell me about my future," he said. "I'm the one who has to work nights to supplement my income. I'm the one in hock up to my ears to finance something I believe in—something I believe is my own divine calling. But I'm not going to hand my cartoons over to you the way everything else in your life has been handed over. You want to do business? Then you think about my terms. And if you decide that we have something further to discuss, you know where to reach me." He started toward the door, but Andi's words stopped him.

"You're proud of yourself, aren't you?" she asked him through tight lips. "You love throwing your poverty at me like it's some elite club I'm not invited to join. Well, wallow in it, then. It's always easier to settle for something, isn't it? As long as you convince yourself that it's your *calling*—" Her words choked off, and she turned her back to him and forced the mist in her eyes to dry. Struggling to rid her face of expression, she stalked back to her desk and closed the file as if the offer was no longer extended. "There are other animators, Justin," she said, but before the words were out of her mouth she remembered a similar threat flung eight years ago. "There are other men," she had said in desperation, grasping at anything that would have kept him from walking out the door.

He remembered, too, and as he had done the last time, he called her bluff. "Then do business with them," he said simply, walking to the door. He stopped halfway out, then turned to voice an afterthought. "And if you do decide to contact me again, I'd appreciate it if you wouldn't call until after ten in the morning. I allow myself four hours of sleep a day, and between six and ten A.M. I don't like to be disturbed." The door slammed behind him, leaving Andi staring after him in silent rage.

Chapter Two

Justin's foul mood had only gotten fouler as he pulled onto his gravel driveway behind the cars of his staff members who were, no doubt, hard at work, while waiting with bated breath to hear how his meeting had gone. He had warned them what his answer would be, but they'd convinced him to go, anyway, and just hear her out.

He went in the screen door on the side of the house and let it slam behind him. Madeline, one of his chief animators, looked up from her work at her drafting table, her black curls bobbing in her big eyes.

"Justin, how'd it go?"

"Justin's back?" he heard from another room, and Gene and B.J., two of the other animators, dashed in. "What happened?" they asked.

He plopped wearily down in a chair and pulled his feet up. "Where's Nathan? I might as well get it all out at once."

"Nathan!" Madeline shouted indelicately. "Justin's back! Get in here!"

Nathan plodded in, three straight pins in his mouth and a handful of sketches to be put on the storyboard. He dropped the sketches on the shelf beneath the board and took the pins out of his mouth. "You're back," he said. "So, has our ship come in?"

Justin blew out a disgusted breath. "No. I told you yesterday that Sherman Enterprises was not going to be our ship. Nothing's changed."

Madeline got up from her table and came around to perch on the arm of the couch. B.J. couldn't stand the suspense. He propped his foot on a stool and leaned his elbow on his knee as he asked Justin, "Did she make you an offer?"

"Yeah, if you want to call it that."

They all kept staring at him, waiting, and when he didn't volunteer it, Madeline asked, "Well, are you going to tell us what it is?"

He shrugged. "I don't see the point. I'm not taking it."

Madeline looked at Gene, who had plopped down on the couch next to her. They both rolled their eyes.

"Buddy, you're gonna have real low morale around here if you don't at least tell us what she said."

"That's right," Nathan told him. "You expect a lot out of us, and none of us has even gotten paid regularly in the past few weeks. Man, we've all got investments in Khaki's Krewe."

Justin rubbed his eyes. "I know you do. You have every right to know." He sat up and leaned his elbows on his knees. "Okay. She wants to buy exclusive rights to the Krewe and use the characters in Promised Land."

"That's great!" Madeline shouted, springing off of her perch. "Do you have any idea what that could do for the cartoons? Can you even imagine how great this is?"

"It's a God thing, man," Gene said. "You know it is. We've been struggling and scraping and sacrificing—we've each had to maintain second jobs to supplement—and every day we sit in here and pray that God will deliver us if he's really calling us to do this. Don't you see, buddy? It's an answer!"

"It's not an answer," Justin said. "God would not answer my prayers through Andi Sherman. You have to trust me on this."

Madeline's face was reddening. "Justin, did you turn her down because of a busted relationship when you were in college? You wouldn't really be that stupid, would you?"

He didn't like being called names, but Madeline had always gotten away with it. "No, it wasn't the relationship. You all know there's no love lost between me and the Shermans, but that wasn't the only thing. She wants absolute control over the characters. You know I can't give her that."

"There's a real important word you should learn before you grow up," Nathan said. "It's 'negotiation.'"

"She wasn't interested in negotiation. She's used to getting her own way."

Madeline breathed a mirthless laugh. "And you're not? Give me a break, Justin. I can just see you two standing there like the characters in that Dr. Seuss book. You know, the ones who refused to get out of each other's way, so they just stood there as cities grew up around them and the world changed . . ."

"I don't have to play this game with her, Madeline. She's out of my life."

"Oh, no," B.J. said as he lowered to a chair and covered the back of his head with his hands. "It *is* about their relationship. We're not going to get paid and all our work is going to keep going to waste on obscure cable channels at two o'clock in the morning, all because of a stupid teenaged romance."

"You guys have no idea what you're talking about!"

"We know that our paychecks are late," Madeline said. "We know that we've hung in here with you for a long time, killing ourselves to meet deadlines for those obscure little cable stations, just knowing that one day God was going to turn everything around. And when he does, you have too much pride to accept it. You beat everything!"

"All right, that's enough," Justin said, storming out of the room. "I have work to do. In fact, we all do."

He left them in the room and slammed into his own bedroom that he sometimes used for an office when he couldn't concentrate in the studio. He looked down at the stuff he'd been working on yesterday. It was a funny gag, one they'd all brainstormed on, but today it seemed dry, lifeless. What would it have been like to see his characters made into three-dimensional creatures, roaming around the park shaking hands with children, singing and dancing on stage . . .

There was no use dwelling on it. It wasn't going to happen. His staff would get over it, if they didn't mutiny first.

Someone knocked on the door, and irritated, he called, "What?"

Madeline opened the door and peeked in. Her face was downcast and still angry. "I've decided to work at home for the rest of the day."

He sighed. "Yeah, it figures. Tell you what. Just tell everybody to go home. If everybody stays, we're going to wind up getting into it again, and I'm just not up to it."

She hesitated at the door. "Justin, if you got some sleep and thought this over, maybe you'd have a clear head. Maybe then you could reconsider."

"My head is as clear as it's going to get," he said. "I'm not giving her the exclusive control of my characters, and that's final."

Madeline didn't have anything to say as she turned and walked away. In a few moments, he heard the others leaving, one by one. Was that the mutiny he'd worried about? he wondered. Was he going to lose his staff if he didn't do something quick? Something that would make a difference?

He got up and went back into the studio, crossed to the storyboard, and pinned up the sketches that Nathan had brought in. Then he went to Madeline's table and worked for a while on the continuity sketches that would take them from one gag to the next. His shoulders ached with the effort, and his head ached with the angry thoughts that kept flitting in and out of his mind.

It was late afternoon when he moved to the couch. He rubbed his eyes and tried to focus on the storyboard mounted on the wall in front of him, representing one scene in the segment he was working on. Fatigue diluted concentration, but he pushed the thought of sleep to the back of his mind, for he simply had too much to do before he left for work at nine that night. He checked his watch. Five o'clock. He wondered if his staff had accomplished anything today or if they'd just spent the hours stewing.

He shouldn't have told them of Andi's offer. What was it to them if someone else owned his characters? They weren't the ones who stood to lose anything. He grabbed a sketch pad and sank back onto the small couch facing the storyboard. Did they think he *liked* living one day at a time? Didn't they know that a true answer to his prayers wouldn't come with Andi Sherman attached? Didn't they realize how important these cartoons would be if he just waited patiently for the right offer, one based on God's terms?

He leaned his head back on the cushions of the couch and crossed an ankle over his knee, propping the pad there. Absently he began to sketch Bucky the rock 'n' roll horse, with a microphone in his hand. Around him grew the figures of the other characters—Khaki Kangaroo; Ned the near-sighted farmer; the bird named Melody; the dowager pigs; the bear named Bull; the Cha-Cha Chickens; and Trudeau the troll. Without any conscious thought, he let his pencil fly across the page, sketching the background buildings and rides of the amusement park. His characters looked right. If only Promised Land weren't synonymous with Andi Sherman.

Andi, he thought, remembering how he'd hated that name when he'd met her in college so many years ago. He wondered if he would have fallen so hopelessly in love with her if he'd known at the outset that she was the daughter of *the* Andrew Sherman. But she, knowing his feelings toward the upper class, had led him to believe she was just another middle-class daughter attending a middle-class college. That deception had been her first mistake. For when he'd discovered who she really was, the seeds of distrust sprouted and grew. But he hadn't been shallow enough or biased enough to let her go for that. He couldn't help recalling the heartrending pull he'd felt toward her regardless of the way her social position had changed things. Despite who she was, he had loved her. *That* had been his mistake.

He turned back the page on his sketch pad and tried with his pencil to recall the almond shape of eyes the color of willow leaves, and the way the light had danced in them today, blatantly revealing the moisture that she hadn't been able to hide. He sketched the soft lines of her nose and the full lips beneath them that he had seen stretched taut with anger on more than one occasion. They had been like that the last time, when he'd made their breakup permanent. She had not groveled or begged when he'd left her then. Instead she had wrapped herself in that cold armor she still wore today. With tears in her eyes, she had made it clear that there were "other fish in the sea," and now he wondered if she'd found anyone else in those eight years. Of course, he told himself. She was not the type to waste away over what might have been. The image of Andi with someone else made his fingers curl into a fist, and his instinctual reaction filled him with unaccountable dread.

His pencil left her face and called up memories of her hair, long, blonde, and silky, shimmering with a multitude of colors when the sun hit it just right. That hair had been part of the power she'd had over him. Thank heaven she had worn it pulled back today.

His eyelids grew heavier as the frustrations released themselves through his pencil, and he studied the sketch, wondering if he'd been responsible for turning her into a strong, beautiful glacier who threatened to freeze or drown anyone who came near. She hadn't been cold when he'd known her before. She had been full of warmth then, and so sweet ...

His eyes drifted shut and the tension seeped from his body. His pencil traced a soft line around the edges of her lips before his hand fell limp as sleep overcame him.

Andi pulled her car into the driveway next to the old frame house where his parents had lived before they died. She'd half expected a zany sign out front, a Beware of Troll warning, or a picture on the door of Khaki in her karate gear, poised for spiritual warfare. Instead, there was nothing to set this house apart from the other ordinary houses on the street, and she wondered if Justin lived in the house he used as a studio.

It seemed impossible that she had lived in the same town with him for two years and not known he was here. But then, Promised Land was so isolated, and she had remained in its cocoon since its plans had begun. It had kept her safe somehow, promising her that life could be everything God intended if only she worked hard enough to make it that way and kept her focus.

The sun was falling behind the paint-peeled structure, and she checked her watch. Five-thirty. It had taken her all day to work out her fury and depression, as well as the alternate terms her board of directors had agreed to so that she could approach Justin Pierce a second time. It hadn't taken much probing to discover why he was so wary of her offer. He had been on his way to success a few years ago when someone very much like her had double-crossed him. They had gotten exclusive rights to his characters, then hired most of his staff out from under him and written him out of the picture. Khaki's Krewe was a new set of characters with a new staff. In light of the circumstances, she didn't blame him for his suspicious attitude. And he had reason to suspect the Sherman name. He had been double-crossed and lied about by her father, and Justin had heard much about her father's ruthless business dealings before he was saved. He probably thought that ruthlessness was genetic. If she was going to work with him, she would have to give a lot more than she'd planned.

When no one answered the front door, Andi left the creaky porch and looked down the side of the house for another entrance. A screen door drew her, and when she had reached it she saw that the door behind it was open as if in invitation. She knocked on the frame, waited, knocked again. When no one came, she cupped her hands around her eyes and peered through the black screen. Her breath caught in her throat when she saw Justin asleep on the couch, a pencil in his hand and a forgotten sketch pad on his lap.

Quietly she opened the screen door and stepped into the studio. For a moment, she stood looking at him, stunned at how good it felt to let her eyes linger over him without that pride between them.

Unbidden memories brought bitter tears to her eyes. She had long ago forgiven her father for his mistake, and her mother for her passive acquiescence, made out of love for their only child. They had never understood that the extremity of their care had helped to rob their daughter of the only man she had ever loved. But that was in the past. Her parents had both come to know Christ at a revival service she'd brought them to several years ago, and she knew that they would never attempt anything so dishonest or manipulative again. Still, her father's offer of a payoff had not been what killed their relationship. It had been her own willingness to believe the worst about Justin.

Breathing a shuddering sigh, she stepped further into the room, smiling at the drawings of Khaki Kangaroo and some of the other characters on the walls sketched from different angles. Clay models of the characters topped some of the shelves above inclined tables cluttered with papers. She went to the storyboard on the wall next to the couch where Justin lay sleeping. The pictures representing each action in the scene gave her a clear idea of the gag the characters were pulling on the troll. Silently she laughed. Justin's talent had always been brilliant.

Well, she thought resolutely, she would have to wake him. It was better to speak with him on his own turf, and since no one else was around, this could be a good opportunity. Besides, there wasn't much time to waste. The park would be opening soon, and they would have to begin working immediately if they were going to incorporate this last-minute addition. She lowered herself onto the couch beside him, careful not to surprise him into wakefulness, and whispered, "Justin."

He stirred slightly but didn't awaken, so she touched his arm. Still there was no response. She studied his face, so serene and relaxed, different from the way it had seemed this morning, but much the same as it had been all those years ago. A shadow of stubble darkened his jaw, and his lips were parted slightly, slow rhythmic breathing whispering through them. His black hair fell into his face, and a strand was caught in the thick dark lashes curling away from his cheek. Without thinking, she raised her hand and pushed the hair from his eye, her fingertips following the soft arch of his brow, the touch again making her aware that her feelings had never died. His face turned into her fingers then, lips brushing lightly against the heel of her hand as he readjusted his head.

The movement stopped her heart, suspended her breath, but she didn't remove her hand. His face was warm with sleep, rough to the touch, and she let her fingers follow the hard, carved lines of his jaw. The impact of sensations bursting through her heart surprised her. Had she been so lonely that a simple touch could confuse her so completely?

Pulling back, she turned sideways on the couch and rested an elbow on the cushions behind her, propping her head as she gazed on the handsome, sleeping man. She had been attracted to men since him, and many had been attracted to her. But since her father's accident there had been no one, for she spent every moment that she wasn't working sitting at his hospital bedside, praying for the moment he would come out of his coma and see that she had carried out the plans for the dream that had become her own. Until now, she hadn't been aware of her need for the touch, the response, of another human being. Sudden loneliness filled and enveloped her.

Unwilling to wake him just yet, she let her eyes linger on his face, on the sound of his breathing, on the man he was without the barriers of pride and memory.

A loud sigh pushed through Justin's lips, and he shifted slightly. The sketch pad that had been lying facedown on his lap slid off and hit the floor.

She jumped.

Closing her eyes and holding her breath until she realized the sound hadn't disturbed him, Andi tried to think rationally. She should run as far away from him as she could. She should send a representative to make her offer, and make sure that their business dealings brought them together as little as possible. But somehow, she couldn't make herself get up and leave. She was caught in a net he didn't even know he had cast.

She looked down at the sketch pad, which had fallen face down, and wondered what he'd been working on. Quietly, she leaned over and picked it up, turned it over . . .

Her heart jolted as her own face stared back at her. Had he been sitting here thinking of her? Sketching her? She studied the rendition, amazed that he hadn't given her horns or a witch's hat, blackened a tooth or drawn a wart or mustache. It was a sweet likeness of her, with sparkling eyes and a coy smile . . .

Her heart raced as she set the pad back on the floor, facedown, so he'd never know she had seen it. Biting her lip, she willed the gnawing in her heart to stop until she could get a proper distance between them and convince herself she didn't still love him . . . that he didn't still love her.

She laid her hand on the couch behind him and watched him, knowing instinctively that she couldn't let him slip away again. She was stronger now, more careful to guard her feelings. She would never let him know of the turmoil he caused within her. But the same God who had allowed them to be torn apart had used a cartoon to hurl them back together. She needed those cartoon characters, and he needed Promised Land. Somehow she would make him see that.

The first step would have to be waking him without letting him know that she'd had a glimpse into his thoughts. Carefully, she got up, made her way across the floor, and slipped out the door. Then she took a deep breath and rapped hard on the wooden door frame. "Hello," she called in her loudest voice, shoving her shaking hands into her pockets. "Is anybody home? Justin?"

The pounding penetrated Justin's sleep, and the voice, urgent and loud, pulled him from the depths of it.

"Justin? Justin?"

He opened his eyes and saw the woman silhouetted against the bright daylight behind her. He squinted as if he didn't believe she was real. Slowly his eyes focused and widened, and he pulled himself up. "I'm coming," he said. He went to the door, his hand shading his eyes from the light as he opened it and let her in. "What time is it?"

Andi checked her watch. "Six o'clock."

"Sorry," he muttered, his hand ruffling his hair distractedly. "I fell asleep." Her penetrating eyes reminded him of the sketch pad he had drawn her picture on, and he went back to the couch and saw that it had fallen on the floor. He picked it up and set it on a table facedown. "I have to work tonight. It's good that you woke me."

He offered Andi a seat on the couch with a wave of his hand, then lowered himself back down, rubbing his eyes.

"When's the last time you slept?" she asked.

He thought a moment, glancing askance at the guarded concern in her eyes, his head leaning indolently against the cushions. "Uh, yesterday morning, I think. Yeah, I got about three hours." His gaze settled on her hands, clamped so tightly that white marks cut through her tan. "What brings you here?" he asked in a voice without that familiar trace of sarcasm. "I thought you decided my cartoons weren't worth the trouble."

She sighed. "You know they're worth it. So my board of directors has been working all day to come up with a compromise—an offer that even you can't refuse."

"A compromise?" A crooked smile played across his face.

"Yes," she said wearily, "I'm willing to compromise in this case. Are you?"

Justin looked down at his knees and rubbed his face again. "That depends on what I have to give up."

"I don't see either of us giving up anything if we can put our past behind us and work together instead of against each other," she said.

He nodded, wishing flashes of the Andi he once knew wouldn't keep surfacing in her eyes, bringing back old feelings despite the chilling aura surrounding her. "I'm listening."

Andi glanced through the door leading further into the house. "Could we talk over coffee? You look like you could use a cup."

"Good idea," he said, standing up. "I can't believe I fell asleep."

"It happens to the best of us, Justin. You should try it on a more regular basis, though."

Brushing past her, he caught her pleasant scent—the long-forgotten scent of a cool breeze across a flowered meadow—as he led her toward the kitchen. The fragrance was familiar . . . too familiar.

He forced himself to block that scent from his mind and led her into the cluttered kitchen. Andi leaned against the kitchen door and watched him spoon the coffee into the pot. Justin plugged in the coffeepot and turned to the table. He pulled out a chair for her. Dropping her gaze, she sat down. He sat across from her and leaned his elbows on the table, hands covering his face.

The coffeepot finished perking, and Justin got up and filled two cups, absently fixing hers the way she had once liked it. He caught himself, then handed her the cup. "Do you still take two spoonsful of sugar?"

She nodded.

Little slips, little slips, he thought. That was how he would lose himself again. He sipped his coffee, watched the steam curling out of it. Bringing his eyes back to hers, he cleared his throat. "So, what's your proposal?"

Andi leaned her elbows on the table and looked into his blue eyes. "I'd like to buy Pierce Productions."

Justin laughed suddenly. "Is that all? Where do I sign?"

Bristling at the sarcasm, Andi tried again. "I expected that reaction, but Justin, give it a chance. For once, just listen."

Attempting to control his amusement, Justin pursed his lips. "For what it's worth," he said in mock acquiescence, "you have my undivided attention."

Andi wet her lips and blew out a frustrated sigh. "I want to make Pierce Productions a part of Promised Land," she said. "You could keep some of the stock and still run the company."

"Under your supervision," he tacked on for her, his eyes still sparkling with amused disbelief.

"Only technically," she said. "You'd have the backing of Promised Land no matter what you did with your cartoons. And nothing would conflict with our interests because we would be ..."

"In control," he provided. "Reaping the profits."

"Profits much higher than you would ever come close to 'reaping' without us," she pointed out. "Promised Land could give you a reputation and credibility. Being under our umbrella could give you infinite opportunities."

"But let's not forget," Justin said, raising a finger, "that Promised Land is under the umbrella of Sherman Enterprises. I'd just be a minute part of the empire."

"Not true," Andi said, unwilling to show her hand but realizing it was the only way to win. "Promised Land is not owned by Sherman Enterprises. *I* own most of the stock in this company. Some of the major stockholders sold out after Dad's accident, and I bought as much as I could. Don't you see that if I bought your company I'd have its best interests at heart? If you succeeded, I'd succeed. And if one of us failed, it would very likely pull the other down. And you know the chances of Promised Land failing."

"Actually," he said, "there have been a hundred times when everybody in town has thought Promised Land would fail. Your fights with the city are almost legendary."

"That's propaganda," she said. "There are people here who have vendettas and will do whatever they can to keep Promised Land from opening. But I've stood up to them, and I always win. Promised Land won't fail, and neither will Pierce Productions if we join forces."

Justin's amusement faded as the offer grew more attractive. "Pierce Productions may not be much," he said solemnly, "but it's mine. I haven't struggled to keep it going all these years just to hand it over to someone else."

Andi pulled a note pad out of her purse and jotted down her first offer. "Does that sound like 'handing it over'?"

Justin read the amount and swallowed. "It doesn't make any difference," he said, resenting the temptation. "I won't work under someone else. I'm not inflexible when it comes to my cartoons, but I'm used to having the last word."

Andi scribbled out the refused offer, then brought her eyes back to Justin, who was watching her with growing interest. "What if I made you president of Pierce Productions, with the stipulation that you could never be fired or demoted in any way and that all creative and management decisions must be approved by you?"

A wry grin crinkled his eyes again, but this time it held less sarcasm. "I already have that."

"But that's *all* you have," Andi said. "With Promised Land's budget you could stretch to the limits of your imagination. You'd have freedom to do anything you wanted, Justin." Sitting back, she waited.

Justin hoped his reeling thoughts weren't apparent on his face. "You have to realize what would be involved here," he said. "For me to make a move like that, I'd want to take my business a lot farther than I've been able to in the past."

"That's the point, Justin. It can take us both farther. Give me some specifics," she said in a voice that had always captivated him. "Think about it for just a minute, and imagine the way you've always dreamed of Pierce Productions."

Justin smiled at her prodding, but he kept his dreams within the realms of reality, knowing that taking the gauntlet meant entering negotiations. "I'd want at least a hundred employees. Most of my work now is done by a pretty small staff, some of whom work out of their homes painting and inking. I'd like to have them all in the same offices, with enough people to work on other projects I have in mind."

"Go on," she said with a grin that was both persuasive and innocent.

"I'd want a sound studio so that we wouldn't have to pay through the nose to use someone else's. And I'd need to update my photographic lab with the most modern equipment."

"Anything else?" she asked, undaunted.

Justin riveted his eyes into hers. "Sixty percent of the stock. I won't give you all of it under any circumstances, and I'd have to have controlling interest."

Andi sat back in her chair. "Justin, that's a lot to ask. I'd have to have at least fifty percent. I won't change my mind on that point." She waited while Justin stared unwaveringly at her across the table. "With fifty percent each we'd be forced to get along. You said yourself that we're both controllers. Well, I don't want to be controlled any more than you do. And, believe me, I have too much responsibility already without having to get very deeply involved in Pierce Productions."

When Justin dropped his eyes in thought, Andi jotted down a higher figure. "This and fifty percent interest."

A competitive grin narrowed his eyes, and he took the pen from her hand and jotted down an even higher figure. "Try *this* and fifty percent interest."

Andi studied the amount for a moment, as if mentally calculating whether it would put too much strain on Promised Land. Of course it would. She'd have to borrow on what was left of her Sherman Enterprises stock. Bringing worried eyes back to Justin, she shook her head. "I probably wouldn't get a return on my investment for over a year, but I'd have to keep feeding money in, Justin. It wouldn't be feasible to pay this much up front."

Justin shrugged and flashed a taunting smile. "You get what you pay for."

Nibbling her lip, Andi stared at the figure again. Justin smiled as if he expected her to withdraw her offer, but she didn't. "All right," she said with resignation. "If we could get into the toy and clothing market within a few months, it might be possible that the investment would be worthwhile." She paused for a moment, thinking, then finally met his eyes. "I guess that means we've got a deal."

"Have we?" he asked with a faint note of surprise. He held her gaze for a long moment, studying her face as he propped his elbow on the back of his chair and inclined his head pensively. For a moment, he thought of backing out, telling her that it still couldn't work, that no matter what she gave him, he wouldn't join forces with her.

But then he remembered the looks on his staff members' faces, the disgust, the anger. And they had a right to be angry. He owed this to them, for their belief in him, their trust that God had gifted and called them, their belief that this was a ministry and a mission. Pierce Productions may be his business, he thought, but if his promises to God had been real, it was God's ministry. Maybe this really was where God wanted it to go.

Finally, he extended his hand, enclosing hers in a handshake more personal than professional. "If my lawyer thinks everything looks right, I guess we can do business," he drawled in a voice deepened to a reluctantly intimate pitch.

"You won't regret it, Justin," she promised. Clearing her throat, Andi disengaged her hand and stood up. "Can you and your attorney be at my office early tomorrow morning?" she asked in a cooler, more pointed voice.

"First thing," he said, his eyes losing their familiar glint and veiling over with the abrupt change in her mood. He pulled himself up slowly, then led her back through the studio to the door, as if the suggestion that she leave was his.

Shuttering her own eyes, she stepped between him and the door's casing. "I hope you'll find some way to get some sleep tonight. You shouldn't enter into an agreement of this sort without rest."

He crossed his arms and leaned against the doorjamb. "-I'll get the weekend guard to relieve me tonight," he said, though he didn't know why he bothered with an explanation. "If all goes well, I won't need that job anymore."

"If all goes well," Andi said, "money will be the least of your problems." Immediately, she regretted that promise, remembering how adamant he had been about denying her money this morning and how delicate the subject of his taking it would be now.

Quietly, he opened the screen door for her.

"Tomorrow," she said, walking away as quickly as she could, refusing to look back at him as he stood in the doorway, silently watching her leave.

When she pulled out of the driveway, Justin let the door bounce shut and went back in to pick up the pad he'd been sketching on before he'd fallen asleep. The incomplete image of the Andi he had once known stared back at him.

Dropping onto the couch, he laid his head back on the cushions and gazed suspiciously at the drawing in his lap, a reminder of how easily a man could be taken in by big green eyes and a captivating smile. But not this time, he vowed. For he was on guard, and awareness would always be the key—the defensive weapon, he believed, that would never slip away.

He set the sketch down and tried to think of all the things he'd have to take care of before morning. A slow, wry grin melted the tension on his face.

"I've got to get a lawyer," he said with a chuckle, and headed for the phone.

Chapter Three

The hospital room was cold, as usual. Andi adjusted her father's covers and stroked back his thinning hair. Andrew Sherman slept, but it wasn't a normal kind of sleep. It was a sleep so deep that nothing and no one could penetrate it.

"Guess who I saw today, Daddy," she said, then glanced over her shoulder at her mother, who sat on the vinyl couch beside the bed, where she spent so much of her life these days.

Georgia Sherman was still a beautiful woman with a Jackie Onassis grace that Andi had always envied, and Andi knew how proud her father would be when he woke to her.

"Who did you see, honey?" her mother asked.

"Justin Pierce," she said. She turned back to her father, searching for a response on his face. "You hear that, Daddy? Justin Pierce."

"Where did you see him?" her mother asked.

She sighed at her father's lack of response and turned back to her mother. "I invited him to the office. We're going to buy his cartoons and make the characters a part of our park."

"Like Mickey Mouse and Goofy?" her mother asked. "That's a wonderful idea. I'm surprised your father didn't think of it."

Andi narrowed her eyes at her mother. "So you have no comment at all about the fact that Justin Pierce is the animator?"

"No, if he's the one you want."

"Not him, Mom. The cartoons."

"Whatever," her mother said with a smile. She patted the vinyl couch next to her, and Andi got up and moved to sit beside her. "Did you tell him your father had tried to find him?"

"It didn't matter, Mom. Justin's still as stubborn as he ever was. He doesn't listen."

"His pride was hurt. So was yours, when he ended things. It takes a lot to overcome wounded pride."

Andi drew in a deep breath and leaned her head back on the edge of the couch. "It shouldn't take so much, Mom. I should be humble and Christlike, but today when I was around Justin I felt my hackles rising. It was like a one-upmanship of lethal blows. How am I going to work with him?"

"You loved him once. Surely there was something you liked about him."

She thought about that for a long moment. "There were lots of things I liked about him. But he wasn't so angry all the time then, so defensive. He had a soft side. And there were a lot of things about me that he liked."

"It's always easier to get along with someone who thinks a lot of you."

Andi smiled, but it quickly faded. "He didn't think much of me today. I guess he hasn't for the past eight years."

"Are you sure about that?"

She thought it over for a moment, and considered telling her mother about the sketch pad with her face on it, but it might not mean a thing, and she hated looking like a pathetic teenager who read volumes into every little thing. "Yes, Mom. I'm sure."

"Maybe you should try asking his forgiveness."

"For what? For believing what my father told me?"

"For believing something that wasn't true about him." She patted Andi's leg. "Honey, maybe he'd feel better about you if you validated his feelings somewhat. Let him know that you understand why and how you hurt him."

"What about *my* feelings, Mom? I was hurt, too. He disappeared for a week. What was I supposed to think? It wasn't my fault—"

"Fine, then. Hold onto your right to be hurt and angry, and he'll hold onto his. 'Love never keeps score.'"

Andi wilted. "When you put it like that . . . I guess I have a lot to learn."

"Don't we all?"

"You don't," she said. Her eyes strayed back to her father. "You've stuck by him, Mom. It's been really sweet to see how you've been here day and night, even when he doesn't know you're here."

"He knows. Somewhere in there, he knows."

"To have a love like that," Andi whispered.

Her mother took her hand and squeezed it. "Most people don't know you'd want that," she said. "You're so independent. So strong. Maybe you need to let your guard down a little more. Put out some signals."

"I don't know," she whispered. "The last time I let my guard down, look what happened. I never want to hurt like that again."

"Sometimes God teaches us through those hurts. What have you learned, Andi?"

She smiled. "To keep my guard up and keep a safe distance between Justin and me."

Georgia took her daughter's face in her hands. "I'm serious."

"Yeah, Mom," Andi said. "So am I."

Chapter Four

The late morning sun outside the boardroom window gave a bright glow to the faces around the bargaining table, and Andi once again let her eyes drift to Justin. He looked rested, and the life and vibrancy that had been so characteristic of him years ago sparkled brightly in his blue eyes as he listened to the two lawyers ironing out the finer points of his merger with Promised Land. Formal negotiations had taken three days of phone calls and lengthy conferences, and now both sides had come together to close the deal. Even after four hours, Justin listened attentively, adding a comment now and then, but generally conveying a positive attitude that Andi found surprising. Was it possible, she wondered, that they could work together amicably and that he would not see her position in the company as one of dictator each time she made a suggestion?

Standing up, she stretched her arms and went to the coffeepot her secretary had kept filled all morning. Tossing a wayward strand of hair back over her shoulder, she poured the black brew into her cup, then glanced back at Justin. His gaze had drifted to her, but the expression in his eyes was hard to read. Telling herself he just wanted coffee, she raised a brow in question and gestured toward the pot in her hand. He nodded.

As the attorneys and various board members continued discussing the details that she had worked out earlier, Andi stepped around them until she stood behind Justin. Careful not to touch his back, she leaned over him and poured. Her hair fell over her shoulder, catching on his. Their eyes met briefly as she swept it back, then he looked down at the cup. Her nerves frayed at his scrutiny of her usually steady hand, and she told herself to get back to her seat as quickly as possible.

She was a fool, she told herself as she slipped back into her chair. And the emotions waging war within her were sure to make it obvious to everyone.

You're a fool, Justin told himself angrily as he watched her settle back into her seat across the table. He shouldn't react to her the way he did, as if he were some kid with a crush on a woman out of his league. She wasn't someone he needed to have on his mind so much. He'd been there, done that. His feeling for her had been a mistake that had taken much too long to recover from. He brought the cup to his lips and glanced at his watch. How much longer would this take? All the points he'd wanted had been covered already. What more was there to talk about?

Again he felt her eyes on him, but he refused to meet them. It was her strategy, he reminded himself. She was merely trying to distract him so that his mind wouldn't be on the details. And the worst part was that it was working.

Unbuttoning the top button of his white shirt and loosening his tie, he forced his mind back to the conversation, hoping that they would at least break for lunch soon. He needed air. He needed distance. He needed time to get his thoughts and senses back in order.

Andi jotted down one of the points that Justin's attorney had just mentioned, noting from the corner of her eye that Justin was unbuttoning his cuffs and rolling his sleeves up. Over an hour ago he had shed his coat and tossed it over the back of the chair next to him. Justin had never liked dressing up. But his attorney had probably advised him to dress for the board members today. Little did he know that the members were so enchanted with his cartoon that he could have worn a Hawaiian muumuu and their opinions would not have swayed.

Taking sympathy with his obvious discomfort, Andi waited for the attorneys to come to the end of one clause in the agreement before she interrupted. "I think that's enough for the morning. Does anyone have any objections to breaking for lunch?"

A breath of relief sounded almost in unison, but none of the strained faces showed more gratitude for the suggestion than Justin's. As the group broke up, Wes slapped Justin on the back. "It's going well, Justin," he said. "I know we'll make a good team."

"I'm counting on it," he said, his eyes drifting past the man to Andi, who was exchanging a few private words with her attorney.

"We'd like to treat you to lunch on the grounds," Wes went on. "We have only one little coffeehouse open for the workers, but the food's not bad. We'd also like to give you a tour this afternoon before we get back to business."

"We?" Justin asked.

"Andi and I."

Andi's eyes flashed alarm at Wes when she heard the exchange. "Justin probably wants to spend some time with Mr. Boteler," she said, referring to his attorney. "I don't think—"

"No problem," Justin's lawyer assured her. "I have to make a few phone calls, and I think a tour will keep him busy while I do that."

As though sensing her discomfort—and delighting in it—Justin shrugged and offered a challenging smile. "I'd love to see the grounds."

Andi recognized the challenge, and was not willing to appear to be backing down from it. Starting out of the conference room, she said, "Meet us in my office when you're ready."

When she and Wes were alone in her office, Andi sat down behind her desk and let her cool, taut facade fade into a hard glare. "I thought *you* were going to take him on the tour," she bit out. "We agreed to that this morning. I told you I have too much work to do."

"You can't avoid him, Andi," Wes said.

"I'm not avoiding him," she said, waving a hand across the stacks of papers on her desk. "I've got too much to do. What makes you think I don't feel comfortable with him, anyway?"

Wes snickered and fished a Tootsie Pop out of his pants pocket. He unwrapped it and stuck it in his mouth. "It's me, Andi. I know you. You're as tense as a kid on her first date when you're around him."

Andi heaved a frustrated sigh and leaned wearily back in her chair, angry that she had let it show so easily. "Wes, I was not tense on my first date. And if I was tense today it was over business, not Justin."

Wes chuckled and pulled up a chair. "Oh yeah, I'd almost forgotten. You weren't tense on your first date because you didn't want to go, did you? I'll never forget that story . . . that your dad picked him out for you and you were determined to make him hate you."

A half smile melted the icy lines on Andi's face at the memory of the prep-school senior who had spent so much energy trying to impress her father. "It was kind of fun convincing him I was a klutz. After I got finished with him, he probably considered it no wonder that my father had to find my dates for me."

"Your father probably wanted to kill you," Wes said on a laugh.

Andi's smile traveled to her eyes. "But he never tried to fix me up again."

"No, I'm sure he didn't," Wes said. "Only *break* you up."

Andi's eyes fell with the expression on her face, and she focused on her laced fingers. "Yes, well." Issuing a deep sigh, she brought her eyes back to her friend. "I really can't take Justin on the tour."

Wes plopped into a chair and regarded Andi with narrowed eyes. "So you're just going to stay clear of him until the first time you have to ask him to do something?"

Realizing what he was getting at, Andi leaned forward on her elbows. "Wes, what's wrong with that? I don't make close friends with everyone on staff. I don't hold their hands and try to convince them that they've made the right decision by joining Promised Land."

"Everyone else is different," Wes contended. "You don't feel the need to walk on eggshells around them. The sooner you get over that with Justin, the sooner we can get down to business."

Andi shook her head and brushed her hair back with stiff fingers, realizing that Wes was right. As president of Promised Land, she would have to get past her feelings for Justin and establish a comfortable working relationship from the beginning. In her head she knew it, but her heart was aware it was on unstable ground. "I didn't exactly dress for getting out today," she said in near surrender, glancing down at the jade dress she had worn for the meeting.

"Neither did we," Wes said with a smile. "It won't hurt for the construction crews to see you dressed like a woman for a change."

Just as she opened her mouth to protest, a knock sounded and Justin walked in, erasing her retort from her mind. He had taken off his tie as she had anticipated, and released a couple more buttons on his shirt. His smile was pleasant yet guarded. Determined not to seem tense, Andi stood abruptly and gestured toward the window. "Are you ready to see what God has done with an impossible dream?" she asked brightly.

In light of the phrasing of her question, Justin could not help but offer a dazzling smile and follow her out of the room.

Chapter Five

The gentle heat of the April sun was a sedative to Justin's coiled muscles as he strode beside Andi along Downtown, Planet Earth, where crews of painters added the artwork that would bring the gift and candy shops to life. His mind still reeled from talking with the "imagineers" who sat at a programming console in the coffeehouse where they had eaten lunch, computer-choreographing the floor show that the robots would perform on stage. They had already begun designs for his characters, who would do automated shows in some of the other coffeehouses across the park, and it was clear that they valued his input on the types of dances and gestures to keep the characters consistent with his cartoons. For the first time since he'd made the decision to accept Andi's offer, Justin was certain he'd done the right thing.

"Most of the rides are finished," Andi was saying as they came to a fork in the road that led to a number of visual magnets. "They would all be ready, except that I kept coming up with new ideas that I thought were essential. Yesterworld was an afterthought," she said with a laugh, waving a hand toward an area in the distance where he could see scaffolding surrounding unfinished structures, and crews busily working. "My board has come close to having me committed a few times, but generally I manage to convince them that my ideas are good ones."

Wes narrowed his eyes. "If I know Andi," he teased, "Promised Land won't ever be finished. There'll always be something new in the works."

"We have the land for it," Andi said with a shrug. "If we have the ideas, why not?"

"And the money?" Justin asked.

Andi lifted her chin and gave him a cool, direct smile. "We get by," she said.

He offered the beginning traces of a smile. "I gather my cartoons were one of those 'afterthoughts'?"

Andi nodded. "I felt something was missing. It took a little doing, but I finally convinced the board that without its own characters, Promised Land was no different from any other amusement park. And Dad's dream was to make it a family event, the best park in the world. If he'd gotten it to this stage, he probably would have had the same idea."

Justin propped a foot on a shaded bench and tilted his head as he smiled at Andi. "You never really said why you liked my characters," he said in a quiet voice, his defenses down for the first time that day.

Andi sat down on the bench and glanced at Wes, who leaned against a tree. "Like I told you, I didn't know they were yours," Andi said. "You never drew kangaroos or trolls in college. I guess the pigs could have clued me in, but even they seemed different back then." Her voice trailed off. "Anyway, I told the board to narrow it down to several choices. They gave me five cartoons, and Khaki's Krewe was one of them. I chose it because it was the best."

"I'm curious," he said. "Would you have even considered Khaki's Krewe if you'd known up front that it was mine?"

"I'm not sure," she said honestly. "But that didn't happen. I chose your cartoon before I ever saw the credits."

He didn't know whether to be flattered or insulted. Had he hoped she had thought of him first when she'd needed an animator? Had he expected her to have given him special favors because of their past? Would he even have wanted her to? For a moment, he struggled with those questions, then finally looked around and asked in a hollow voice, "Where d'you want to go next?"

Andi seemed relieved at his dismissal of the subject, and she pointed to the next ride.

Justin refused to let her all-business manner ruin his day, and as she and Wes escorted him through the park, he saw her slipping out of her ice casing from time to time as they walked beside waterless canals and steep roller coaster tracks.

Forgetting her inhibitions as she shared her world with him, Andi captured his complete attention as she expounded on the history of each ride—which had been her father's brainchild, which had been her own. The attention to detail intrigued Justin—from the painted garbage cans in the shapes of miniature houses to the blinking and "breathing" wax figures of legendary Bible heroes in the Hall of Faith.

Even the more practical side of the park in the underground service and utility basement fascinated him. As the executive engineer explained the technical aspects of the park and the computer center that would keep things operational, Justin began to get more excited than he had ever been about the future he saw for himself and his characters.

After a while Wes excused himself to take care of some problems that had come up in the construction on one of the rides. Andi led Justin back into the sunshine, watching his face for the wonder and thought that had colored it during the tour. Seeing her visions reflected back in Justin's eyes reminded her of all the plans they'd shared when they were in college. She wondered if he was reminded of the same thing.

Andi led him into the castle that served as the focal point of the park, up the winding staircase and into the bell tower, from which they had a 360-degree view of the park. "Impressed?" she asked with a perceptive smile as he made a slow turn and took in the majesty of his surroundings.

Justin leaned back against the rail facing her, unable to control his grin. "What do you think?"

Andi's soft laughter played like a melody on the wind. "I think if you were, you'd never admit it."

His grin grew broader. "That's where you're wrong. I admit it." Turning his back to her, he leaned on his elbows and scanned the colorful landscape, letting the wind ruffle through his hair and clear his mind. "I always knew you'd do something big, Andi."

Andi went to stand beside him. "I wasn't going for size, Justin. I was going for impact."

"Well, you're making one. I'm kind of going for impact, myself. I wonder if our two impacts will clash, or just make a bigger impact."

"If you don't see the possibilities here, Justin, then you're not dreaming as big as you used to."

He chuckled. "Some dreams are more realistic than others, Andi."

"Realistic dreams. Hmm. Isn't that a contradiction?"

"Not for me. I've worked hard for everything I've ever gotten, Andi. Real hard."

She met his eyes, and that old anger began to rise again. "It may come as a surprise to you, Justin, but so have I."

"Sure, you have, Andi. But you had something to start with."

"I had money, and you had talent. We were each very blessed. I hope you haven't become a snob, Justin."

"A snob? What is that supposed to mean?"

"You know the definition of 'snob.' I'm beginning to think that you have nothing but contempt for anyone with money. But I don't make any apology for having it."

"I'm not a snob." Justin leaned on a column and gazed out across the panoramic view below him, his heart deflated by his own hand. How in the world would he get through this madness? When would he stop trying to get the last word? When would he quit looking for comebacks to everything she said?

"There's Wes," Andi said, her voice hoarse with dejection as she pointed to an electric car traveling toward the tower. "I guess we'd better get back."

Justin followed her down the staircase, fighting his need to call a truce with her. The truth was, he doubted one would hold, anyway.

When Andi was at the wheel of the small, noiseless car and they were driving back toward the office building, Justin looked over at her, sensing the tension in her face as she squinted into the sun to see a crowd of workers forming near the Jacob's Ladder ride. Looking ahead, Justin could see two men shouting at one another. The others were scattered, watching the scene. Andi bit the inside of her lip, and her eyes glowered with anger Justin recognized but did not understand. She stopped the car in front of the crowd, and without offering a word in explanation, jumped out and rushed through the men, who parted at her presence.

Justin glanced back at Wes. "What's going on?"

Wes leaned casually back in his seat. "Just a few little kinks to work out. Andi can take care of it."

He watched Andi face off with one of the men, hands on her hips. In any other situation, a construction crew would have been making catcalls at the long-haired beauty who marched so dominantly into their territory. The only evidence Justin could see of anything other than the greatest respect for her was an occasional nudge between two men or the private way one here or there shook his head in appreciation of her beauty.

Wes sat up and pointed toward one of the men. "That's one of the parish building inspectors. Starts an uproar almost every time he comes in here. He's convinced we're going to substitute cardboard for lumber one of these days."

"The parish building inspector?" Justin asked, shifting in his seat to see Wes better. "Didn't I read that Promised Land was self-governing? I didn't think it was under the parish's jurisdiction."

"We're self-governing, all right, just like Disney World is. We're set up just like our own town. Andi fought for that with everything she had, and finally the state legislature agreed. But the town officials like to think they still have their hands in. Andi gave them the gratuitous right to send inspectors in, hoping that when they saw that she was using higher standards than they did, they'd realize our structures were safe and would leave her alone. Unfortunately, they're determined to find something wrong and report it to the press. They want to start a panic that will keep us from opening on time."

Andi disappeared inside the building with the two arguing men, and the other workers relaxed their stances a bit, talking quietly among themselves. "Shouldn't you be taking care of this?" Justin asked, uncomfortable at the thought of her alone with them.

Wes shrugged. "I've butted heads with them already this morning—if I get into it again it might come to blows. Besides, the builder for this part is right there. I coordinate all of the building overall, but I have to let each builder fight his own battles with the inspectors. Unless Andi wants to get involved, that is. She's the president and CEO. Can't get any higher than that." He laughed. "Besides, I don't like to be around when she's on the rampage."

A few more moments went by, and Justin felt his muscles thicken with tension. Nervously, he brushed his bottom lip with his finger. "What are they doing in there?"

"Probably pulling out nails to prove they used the right size or showing the idiot the paint to prove it doesn't have a lead base—some such nonsense."

"Andi has to keep up with all that?"

Wes gave a hoarse chuckle. "Andi keeps up with everything. She spends most of her time out here with these men. Even if one of our contractors wanted to slip in low-grade materials, they wouldn't get past both of us. Andi doesn't take chances, and she intends to settle the inspectors' minds before she opens this park."

Andi came back out of the building followed by the two men, who seemed calmer now. Her face was still tight and authoritative, and without another word, she got back into the car and started it.

"Everything all right?" Justin asked.

"Just fine," she bit out. "Everything's just great. Givens sent him in here to get a sample of one of the rafters. Said one of his reporters got a tip that it was green wood."

B.W. Givens, Justin thought. The man who owned Shreveport's newspaper and one of the television stations, and who had most of the town's government in his pocket. The man who had made no secret that he planned to find a reason to keep the park from opening. The man whose propaganda had stirred the community into an uproar over the belief that Promised Land was certain to ruin the area. Stretching his arm across the back of her seat, Justin could almost feel the cold radiating from her.

As they parted on the twentieth floor so that Justin could confer with his attorney before the meeting began again, Andi was polite but distant. He watched thoughtfully as Wes followed her to her office, and suddenly he was filled with a deep, sinking feeling that he was no longer foremost in her mind. She had concerns and obligations that went far beyond whether or not the two of them still felt the old stirrings. The realization was disappointing, for it had somehow been rewarding to think that her primary concern, for a while, was him.

The shift in her interest left him cold and empty, for a memory plagued him, a memory of her eyes brightening at the mere sight of him, a memory of her every action having some relationship to him, a memory of love so strong that it had seemed ordained. But memories were no more than unattainable dreams, he reminded himself. And the yearnings that had been plaguing him since he'd first seen her a few days ago were just temporary results of surprise and fatigue. Somehow he would shake them.

He would not let her under his skin again.

Chapter Six

The night sky outside Andi's office window was bold and beautiful, reminding her that there was life outside Promised Land. Lately she had been working too hard and worrying too much. The days were never long enough for all she had to do, but the excitement of watching God's work unfold before her eyes was all the motivation she needed. It escaped her how the employees of Promised Land could simply walk away at the end of the day when there were so many important things yet to be done. Even when she was tired, emotionally drained, and a little depressed as she was now, she found it difficult to leave.

She wondered if Justin would feel that way.

His coolness toward her in the meeting that afternoon had contributed to her mood, giving her just one more reason to want to get back to her desk and bury herself in busywork. She'd been aggravated enough after her confrontation with the lunatic building inspector, so Justin's change in attitude after their almost amicable afternoon had only served to vex her more. One step forward, two steps backward. But he hadn't found fault with her park, she thought with a faint smile. She was certain he had tried, but instead he had understood her dream. For a moment their minds had met and shared her vision. His admiration had been clear. That, in itself, was endearing.

Discarding the bagged remains of her dinner, Andi stood up and stretched, realizing that she owed herself a little relaxation. After all, they had closed the deal today and that deserved celebration. If nothing else, she could at least knock off now and go to the hospital early to sit with her father. The work would still be there tomorrow, and she was unlikely to put even a dent in it tonight.

Closing her office door behind her, Andi saw that the light of the boardroom was still on. She stepped quietly across the plush carpet and peered in the doorway. Wes sat at the table, a million papers spread out in front of him along with blueprints and charts depicting the amount of technical work left to be done. "Did you clutter yourself out of your office?" she asked with a smile.

Wes looked up. "I needed more room to spread out," he said.

Andi grinned. "That's why we put a long table in your office."

"It was covered with something else I was working on. I didn't want to lose anything by moving it."

Andi laughed softly and stepped inside the boardroom, setting her briefcase on the table. "Why don't you wind it up, Wes? It's late and it's been a long day."

"A day that kept me from getting any real work done," he muttered. "Besides, the only time it gets quiet enough to work is when it's late. I'm staying. It's okay, though. Laney and Amy are out of town tonight on a church choir trip. They won't miss me. I have to admit, I'm a little worried about her traveling while she's pregnant. The work keeps my mind off of it."

"All right," she said, picking up her briefcase and starting out. "I'll see you tomorrow, then."

"Where are you going?" His voice came a little too anxiously, and she turned back.

"To the hospital."

His eyebrows buckled, and he scrubbed his chin. "I thought as much. Andi, you need to rest. Don't you think your father could get by without you there one night?"

"Sure, he could," she said. "But I don't sit with Dad because someone needs to. Mom's there with him a few hours a day. He doesn't even know we're there. I just want to be with him."

Wes pushed out of his chair and stood up, leaning over the table with a look of no-nonsense conviction on his tanned face.

"Andi, you need to get out more, spend some time with people."

"I do that all day," Andi protested.

"I mean friends. You spend so much time here that you don't have a social life. You're not taking very good care of yourself."

She dropped into a chair and wilted at the table. "Well, it's not like I have friends coming out of my ears. It isn't like in college."

"College is just a preparation time for real life, Andi. You can't repeat it. But you can make things better."

She looked at him for a moment, trying to decide why he would pick today to say that to her. "Wes, if you think I've been dwelling on college days, you're wrong. You're reading way too much into my joining forces with Justin. I'm really not trying to start things up with him again. He walked out on me once, and I don't intend to give him the chance to do it again."

"I know that. I didn't mean that at all. But you need fellowship, Andi. You need encouragement. You need people. Maybe people who don't work for you."

"I have a church."

"Yeah, but it happens to be on the grounds of Promised Land, and the only people who worship there yet are your employees. It's not the same."

"That'll change. When the park opens, and people start coming—"

"I'm talking about *now*, Andi. How can you stay in tune with God when you're hanging there all alone?"

"All God's instruments are a little out of tune, aren't they?" she asked with a half-smile.

"They don't have to be. I have a theory," Wes said, sitting back in his chair and crossing his legs. "Want to hear it?"

"Sure."

"My theory is that God is using both of you, but you're both letting the busyness of his work keep you from any real fellowship with him. Maybe he brought you both back together here to encourage each other. Maybe to renew that intensity you both had back in college."

"Interesting theory," Andi said. "But probably wrong. Justin's not interested in encouragement from me. And he has plenty of intensity. So do I."

"Maybe it's not for the right things."

She looked across the table at him, then smiled softly. "You may be right about that."

"Iron sharpens iron, remember?"

"Yeah, but the sharper it is, the more dangerous it is." She slid back her chair and got up, sighing from her soul. "Look, don't worry about me. I'll see you tomorrow, okay?" With the last words, she went through the doorway, but Wes stopped her again.

"Did you know Justin left his coat and tie here today? I wonder if he'll need it tomorrow. He's not the type to own two suits."

Andi glanced at the coat still draped over the back of the chair and the tie crumpled in a heap on the seat. "No, I'm sure he doesn't," she said, going back in and picking them up, unconsciously smoothing the fabric over her arm as she set her briefcase down again. "But I'm also sure he doesn't plan to wear it tomorrow."

"I don't know," Wes objected. "If I read him right, he'll be out first thing tomorrow getting things set up for the move, ordering new equipment, doing some banking ..."

Andi gave Wes a knowing grin and he answered it, no longer trying to hide his ulterior motives.

"Take him his coat, Andi," he said. "Talk to him. Make friends with him, if nothing else."

Andi wasn't fooled. "But *something* else is more what you had in mind, isn't it, Wes?"

Wes shrugged and attempted an innocent smile. "Can't blame a guy for trying."

Pensively, Andi dropped her gaze to the coat and tie, and she wondered if they smelled like Justin. A sudden warmth washed through her, making her uneasy. "I was considering having a press conference tomorrow to announce that he's joined us," she said without meeting Wes's eyes. "A reception, maybe. The press people love those. Do you think it's too short notice?"

"Go invite him!" Wes enthused, giving a that's-the-spirit punch at the air. "No notice is too short for the press. They're starved for news on Promised Land. Go take him his coat and invite him. You'll have two excuses."

"This may come as a shock to you," Andi retorted mildly, "but I wasn't looking for an excuse to see Justin."

"But you'll go?"

"Maybe," she said. "I'll let you know." Again, she got her briefcase and started out of the room, turning back at the threshold. "And Wes? Thanks for caring."

Quirking his lips, he said, "Somebody has to do it." Then, as if the exchange had never taken place, he bent back over his work as Andi shook her head and left the room.

It was difficult finding Justin's house in the dark, but at last Andi picked it out and pulled into the driveway. Two cars were parked ambiguously on the street between his house and the one next door—making her uncertain if he had visitors or if his neighbors did—but the lack of lighting, except for the faint yellow one through the front curtains, gave the impression of inactivity.

An instant of cowardice flitted through her mind and almost made her reconsider. Why *had* she come? Wasn't she just making herself an open target for pain? She picked the coat up, squeezed the fabric in hands that trembled slightly, then brought it to her face. It *did* smell of him, clean yet exotic, the same unique scent he had worn years ago. Funny how she had never forgotten that smell.

Draping the coat and tie over her arm, she walked over the lawn still soft from the last rain and went up the porch steps leading to his front door. Swallowing back her fear, she rang the bell.

The vibration of footsteps on the hollow wooded floor told her someone was coming. She braced herself and mentally rehearsed her greeting. But when the door opened, it was not Justin who confronted her but a petite brunette with spaniel eyes and a smile that seemed on the verge of laughter. "Can I help you?" she asked, pushing back the riotous curls that were slightly subdued by the bright scarf tied in a bow at the top of her head.

Feeling foolish with the coat and tie over her arm, Andi tried to find her voice. "Hi. I'm—"

"Who is it, Madeline?" she heard Justin call as he came up the hall.

The woman stepped back as Justin approached the door in his usual jeans and T-shirt. He probably couldn't wait to get out of that dress shirt today, she mused.

"Andi." His eyes widened in surprise. "I wasn't expecting—"

"I know," she cut in, suddenly regretting the whim that had brought her here and vowing never to take Wes's advice again. "I wouldn't have just dropped in like this, but you left your coat and tie in the boardroom and I—"

"Come in," he said, but Andi shook her head, a dappled pink flushing her cheeks.

"I can't. I just wanted to bring this by." Awkwardly she held out the arm over which the coat and tie were draped.

"Is it the pizza?" a man's voice called from the kitchen.

Justin's eyes locked intimately, almost apologetically, with Andi's, and he reached out and took the coat off her arm. From somewhere deep in the house she could hear music and other voices, and another man appeared behind Justin. "Nope, not pizza," he said.

"We were having a little celebration," Justin said quietly, leaning toward her as if blocking out the others. Lowering his voice to an almost whisper, he said, "Please come in. I want you to meet my staff."

Feeling that a refusal would cause more of a scene than simply stepping inside for a moment, she acquiesced. "I really don't want to interrupt your celebration." She glanced at the other two men who had drifted curiously into the living room.

Justin gave her a soft smile, the first truly soft smile he'd given her in years. "This is Andi Sherman, everybody," he rumbled softly.

With subdued smiles, as if they were in the presence of the wizard who had granted them passage home, they stepped up one by one to shake her hand. Madeline, with her pixie smile, and B.J. and Nathan and Gene.

"As you've heard, we're waiting for pizza," Justin said. "You could help us eat it."

The thought of kicking off her shoes and relaxing with these people who seemed so comfortable around each other was more appealing to her than she wanted to admit, but they were *his* friends, not hers, and it was *his* celebration, and she was quite sure that the invitation had been extended out of politeness. He would probably be horrified if she took him up on it.

"No, I really can't. I have to go. It was nice meeting all of you." She started toward the door, and Justin followed her out into the darkness, his back dismissing the others. Leaning his wrist on the jamb beside his head, he gazed down at her, stopping her heart. Starlight glimmered in his eyes, a radiant heat with more power than Andi remembered. She forced herself to meet his gaze directly. "I'd like to give a press party tomorrow night to announce our merger," she said quickly. "Can you be there?"

Justin shrugged. "Sure."

"Good," she said, taking a step backward. "It'll be formal. You'll have to wear a tux."

"That shouldn't be a problem."

Andi glanced toward her car to hide the awkward look she knew was apparent on her face. "Well, then I'll see you tomorrow night—at seven—if I don't see you before."

"You might," he said. "We'll be in and out of the offices all day tomorrow." When he made no effort to say more, Andi started down the porch steps, but his voice stopped her. "Sure you won't stay for a while?"

Andi breathed a silent, frustrated laugh at the possibility and shook her head. "I can't."

"Where do you have to be?" came the next unexpected question.

Andi dropped her eyes. "The hospital."

"Oh." She wished instantly that she hadn't said it, for she hated his sympathy. That was not what she wanted from Justin.

"Well," she said with an exaggeratedly light sigh, "I guess I'll be seeing you tomorrow night, then. I'm looking forward to doing business with you, Justin."

"So am I," he said, so quietly that she almost couldn't hear.

Wrenching her eyes from his, she started across the lawn.

"Andi," he called through the night breeze.

Andi stopped and turned slowly back to him again, holding her hair back from her face as the wind waged war with it. He didn't speak for a moment, and she felt like a deer caught in the headlights, unable to move until he unlocked his gaze. "Thanks for bringing the coat over," he said finally.

Nodding, Andi got in her car and cranked the engine. Flicking on the headlights that she knew would blind him to her, she let her eyes steal back to him, leaning pensively in the doorway.

Loneliness gripped her and refused to let go as she drove the distance to the hospital, where the other man she had loved and lost lay in wait.

Chapter Seven

The hospital room was still too cold as Andi stepped in, so she went to the closet and found another blanket for her father. Carefully, she laid it over him, tucked it around him, and leaned over to kiss him. "Hi, Daddy. It's me, Andi."

There was no answer, just her father's blank stare. She sat down in the chair beside his bed and stroked his hair back from his forehead. He had gotten a haircut today, she realized. Her mother must have done it.

"Daddy, we signed all the papers today. The cartoon characters I told you about, Khaki's Krewe, are part of Promised Land now. I think they're going to add so much. I wish you could see one of the cartoons yourself. You'd love them."

Her voice fell on deaf ears, for all she knew. Leaning both elbows on the bed, she gazed down at her father, wishing from the bottom of her heart that she could somehow snap him out of this trap he was in. She reached for his hand, laid across his stomach, and squeezed, wishing, praying, that he would squeeze back. If she just had a sign.

But there was no sign.

"Are you even in there, Daddy?" she asked helplessly. "If you were, couldn't you tell me somehow? I really miss you."

She waited, hoping for a sign—a squeeze of the hand, a blink, a change in his breathing pattern—but there was none. Finally, she let go of his hand and sat back in her chair. She felt tired . . . so tired. It was as if she hadn't slept in days, and something inside her felt empty, weak. Where was the joy Christians were supposed to feel? Where was the hope?

Her tear-filled eyes found her father's Bible, where her mother had laid it beside his bed. She had been reading it to him. Since his accident, her mother had read aloud all the way to Habakkuk. She hoped her father could hear, that it brought him some pleasure, some relief.

She picked up the Bible and opened it. Her father's own notes were written in the margins of almost every page, verses were underlined, passages highlighted. Her eyes fell to the passage on the page the Bible had opened to, in the first chapter of James.

"Consider it pure joy, my brothers, whenever you face trials of many kinds, because you know that the testing of your faith develops perseverance. Perseverance must finish its work so that you may be mature and complete, not lacking anything."

She'd read the passage herself, many times, but tonight she saw her father's notes winding around the margins of the page. She turned the Bible sideways and read what he'd written.

"We should consider our personal trials and sorrows joy because of what they can allow God to do in us. If we let our trials break us, God can't use us. But if we go in to those trials knowing that God is going to do something great with us, something for which he has to strengthen us in advance, it all comes into perspective." Then he had jotted, "Romans 8:28."

She didn't have to look that up. It was one of her favorite verses. Aloud, she whispered, "And we know that in all things God works for the good of those who love him, who have been called according to his purpose."

The words from the Bible, along with her father's words, and his cross-reference, all combined to wash a wave of comfort over her. Tears filled her eyes, and she caught her breath on a sob. Was this the sign she had looked for? Had her father written that passage just for her, knowing that one day he couldn't tell her himself?

Probably not. But another of her fathers had known. God had led her to it tonight.

"It's hard to consider it joy," she whispered to God as she read back over the passage. "But when I think it's all for good, that there's a reason, that you have a plan ... it's easier." She dropped her forehead on the edge of the bed, and fell deeper into her tears as she closed her eyes and tried to pray. "Lord, help me. I don't want to be alone, and I am. And nothing seems to be working out ..."

Another verse that had once been dear to her came to her mind. *"But seek first his kingdom and his righteousness, and all these things will be given to you as well."*

That was it. She had not been seeking the kingdom of God first. It had come somewhere down her priority list, after the problems with the building of the park and staving off the government officials, but somewhere before relationships and recreation. Here she was so encumbered with busyness, most of which she called God's work, and ignoring him completely. Closing her eyes, she whispered, "Forgive me, Lord."

She tried to list off the things she needed to repent of: pride, arrogance, neglect, apathy ... "Daddy," she whispered, "how does God keep his patience with me?"

Her father didn't respond, but it was okay, because the peace that came over her told her that her heavenly Father did. She got up, pressed a kiss on her father's temple, and whispered, "Good night, Daddy."

Quietly, she slipped from his room, and headed back to her apartment on the grounds of Promised Land.

Chapter Eight

Justin had expected to run into Andi when he'd shown up at the Promised Land office building the next day, but she had been too obviously scarce. His disappointment surprised and angered him, for he didn't want to spend every moment at work wishing she'd come through the door. That wasn't productive. Besides, if she did, they would only fight, or have one of those stiff conversations packed full of double meanings and barbs that were left to hang. Was that what he wanted? To see her so she could get his adrenaline pumping?

No, that wasn't why. He knew that as clearly as he knew that his merger with her had been a great idea. But he wanted to admit neither.

He had finally gotten most of his stuff moved into the building when he realized that the time was sneaking up on him. While his staff was in his living room—formerly his studio—discussing where they would all eat that evening, he had slipped away to take a shower.

He had plenty of time, he told himself, and as he dressed in the silly tuxedo shirt he'd rented earlier that day, he wished that he could appear at the reception as himself—in jeans and sneakers. But being part of corporate America meant making a few concessions, he supposed. He tucked the shirt in, put on his cummerbund, and wondered who had invented a getup like this. It was neither practical nor reasonable, and he felt like a clown dressing in it now. He looked down at the limp tie in his hand, and wondered how in the world he would tie it.

"Madeline!" he yelled through the door.

"Yeah!" she shouted back.

"Come give me a hand with this blasted tie, will you?"

Madeline came around the corner, her curls bouncing in her face, and she laughed out loud at the sight of him. "I never thought I'd see the day!" she said. "You look like a million bucks. Guys!" she shouted. "Come get a load of this!"

The others filled the doorway quickly, mocking him with catcalls and whoops. "I told you," Madeline teased. "You're lookin' good."

He shot them looks that said he wasn't buying. "Can you tie this tie? It's too short. I can't figure out—"

"It's a bow tie, Einstein. Here, let me do it." Mechanically, she began to tie the tie. "I didn't have three brothers for nothing, you know. Andi's gonna swoon, Justin. The minute she lays eyes on you, she's just gonna swoon."

"Andi's never swooned in her life," he said irritably.

"You watch. When you walk in, she'll have to grab onto something." She demonstrated by grabbing onto a chair. "Her eyes will roll back up in her head. Her face will turn pink, and she'll stumble back ..."

He laughed as she pretended to faint, then caught herself. "Now when she does it, Justin, you have to get right over there and catch her. It's the only gentlemanly thing to do."

Still laughing, he checked the tie in the mirror, wishing he could loosen it a little. "You sure don't know Andi Sherman."

"Justin, I'm a woman. I see things that you can't. I saw the look on Andi's face last night when she was here. This relationship may have been dormant for eight years, but it's not dead for her, either."

"Either?" he asked. "What do you mean, 'either'?"

She chuckled. "I mean that I think the feeling is mutual. I've never seen two people more enamored of each other, yet putting on such a front. Who are you trying to kid, anyway? She's knock-dead gorgeous, she's generous, she's sweet . . . and you were in love with her once. My money says you still are."

"Yeah, well, your money is weak with anemia. It's not thinking clearly."

"Not true. I injected it today with that fat check you gave me." Giggling, she started out of the room. "We're heading out to eat. Have fun at the reception."

"Yeah, big fun," he said without much hope.

He heard them all milling out of the house, the door closing behind them. He checked his watch. He was running forty-five minutes early, but he figured it wouldn't hurt to get there early, hang around in his new studio for a while, and get his ducks all in a row. He had to admit he was a little nervous. He had never done a press conference/reception before, and he sure didn't want to look like a bumbling fool around Andi.

He looked for his keys, found them in his jeans pocket lying over a chair, and pulled them out. He checked to see if he'd forgotten anything, then stepped out of the side door.

Absent-mindedly, he unlocked the door to his car and started to get in, when he realized that there were three cars in the driveway behind him, blocking him in. They had all left in the fourth.

"Oh, no!" He walked down the driveway to see if he could catch them.

They were already out of his sight.

He raked both hands through his hair and went back inside, grabbed the phone book, and started trying to decide where they might have gone.

Ten phone calls and half an hour later, he had still not found them, and he realized that he wasn't going to. He tried calling Andi, but she wasn't in her office.

Finally, he flipped through the yellow pages to the listing of taxi services, and called the first one on the list. The line was busy.

Banging a fist on the table in frustration, he tried to think. Wes. He could call Wes. Maybe he hadn't left home yet and could give him a ride.

He punched out Wes's number and fidgeted through three rings. A woman answered.

"Hello?"

"Is Wes there, please?"

"No, I'm sorry. He left a little while ago for the reception tonight."

"Laney?"

"No, she went with him. I'm his sister, Sherry."

"Sherry?" Justin laughed. He hadn't seen her since Wes's wedding, and it had been years even before that. "Sherry, this is Justin Pierce. How's it going?"

"Justin!" she shouted. "It's great to hear your voice!"

He grinned. "Listen, I've got a little problem. Are you busy right now?"

"Amy and Clint and I are just hanging around. We're baby-sitting."

He knew Amy was Wes's seven-year-old daughter. "Who's Clint?"

"Well ... Clint's a very interesting, good-looking man who happens to be crazy about me."

Justin heard him laughing in the background.

"I'd invite you over to meet him, but aren't you supposed to be at that reception?"

"Yes. That's my problem. My car is sort of blocked in. If I pay you a million dollars, Sherry, would you come and pick me up and take me to Promised Land?"

"A million dollars, huh? I suppose you'd want to use a credit card."

"Yeah. An expired one."

She chuckled. "All right. Give me directions and we'll be right over."

"Can you hurry? I'm late."

"For a million dollars on an expired credit card, we can be there in five minutes."

Feeling like an idiot waiting out beside the curb in his tuxedo, Justin began to wonder if God was trying to teach him something. His own father had often told him he was "too big for his britches," and maybe this was the Lord's way of saying the same thing. All dressed up with his loaded bank account and a future that looked brighter than it ever had before, and he didn't even have a ride to the party in his honor.

True to her word, Sherry and Clint and Wes's beautiful eight-year-old daughter showed up a few minutes later, and Justin jumped into the backseat. "Thanks, you guys."

Sherry wrenched her neck around and gave him a once-over. "Who are you and what have you done with Justin Pierce?"

Justin grinned. "It's me. Really."

"No," Sherry said. "The Justin Pierce I remember would never have put on a tux." She shifted the car into drive and pulled back out on the street. "Justin, this is Clint Jessup."

Clint reached back over the seat and took his hand. "Good to meet you, Justin. So whose cars are blocking you in?"

"My staff. They're trying to drive me insane." He looked at Amy, who sat beside him staring at him with fascination. "Tell me, do I look insane?" he asked.

She grinned. "You look nice. Were you really my daddy's roommate?"

"Sure was. Where do you think my insanity started?"

He leaned up to the front seat and peered through the windshield. "Can you make this thing go any faster?"

"I'm driving as fast as I can, Justin. But don't sweat it. You'll make an entrance. They'll love you. Besides, you've already signed the contract. What are they gonna do? Fire you?"

He smiled and tried to let that reality relax him, but his tension only coiled itself tighter as they reached the grounds of Promised Land. He thanked them and raced inside.

The chatter of the reporters rambling around the room in clothes they'd rented or purchased just for the occasion grew louder as the night wore on. Conjecture about the nature of Andi's announcement dominated most of the conversations around the room, but those reporters who had been the targets of leaks kept the news to themselves, hoping that only they would be well researched enough to ask the questions that mattered.

Andi Sherman moved from one cluster to another, keeping the conversation at a gossipy pitch. Her perfectly coifed French twist was an elegant contrast to the simple black gown she wore with a regal air. Her smile was a bit too forced, her eyes a bit too distant, but her aloofness was part of her appeal to the media, who kept her as the center of their attention no matter where she stood in the room.

Inwardly, Andi was anything but cool, for her blood seethed through her veins with alarming speed, and it took every ounce of decorum to counter the telltale signs of her fury. Her teeth did not grind together, her knuckles were not white, and the crystal glass in her hand did not crumble in her grasp. But she knew that the moment Justin Pierce came through that door her reserve would come crashing down in rage around her.

She fumed inwardly as she worked her way to the entrance of the plush suite. He had known he was the subject of the announcement. In fact, he knew that the whole function was in his honor! As thanks he had left her to placate these reporters, hungry more for the story of the hour than for the food and punch she kept circulating. Even B.W. Givens, who owned half the town and was determined to keep Promised Land from being part of it, was in attendance, watching and waiting with vulturelike shrewdness for some sign of trouble in Promised Land.

For the thousandth time in a quarter of an hour, Andi doubted the wisdom of her agreement with Justin. She had obviously been too easy. As Wes had pointed out yesterday, she had spent too much time walking on eggshells around him. But that was about to come to an end.

Behind her, Laney Grayson whispered, "Calm down, Andi. He'll be here."

Andi still had her smile pasted on as she turned around to Wes's wife. Laney was seven months pregnant, but still looked as elegant as she had before she'd ever begun to show. "It's a little embarrassing," Andi whispered impatiently.

As Wes joined them, Laney said, "Well, if it helps any, it doesn't show. Does it, Wes?"

"Nope. You look as calm and collected as a deodorant model."

If she hadn't been so angry, Andi might have appreciated his attempt to make her laugh. "Thanks, Wes. You're a real prince."

The elevator smoothed to a stop on the nineteenth floor of the office building, and Justin checked his watch as he lurched out and rushed toward the party that awaited him. "Blazes," he muttered when he saw how late he was. Sherry Grayson had an authority complex and insisted on driving the speed limit. It beat anything he'd ever seen.

He tugged at his stiff collar and strangling bow tie before jogging toward the noise coming from down the corridor.

Justin had scarcely reached the open double oak doors of the noisy suite when he saw Andi near it, a glacial, untouchable vision of loveliness. She looked up at him and their eyes collided. She was angry. Her frigid eyes riveted scornfully into him as she excused herself from a reporter and pushed out to the hall.

The very look on her face riled him, and he stiffened, deciding not to let those crystal daggers in her eyes get the best of him. If he'd had any plans of apologizing to her, or offering an explanation, he changed his mind now and took on his most defensive facade. He may have merged companies with her, but he would not let her treat him like an inept employee. He met her expression with one equally hard, equally haughty.

She grabbed his elbow and began to pull him toward a secluded wing. "How dare you?" she asked when they were out of earshot of the press.

"How dare I what?"

"How dare you waltz in here fifteen minutes late? I got these people here for you. They're getting restless, and I don't think I need to remind you how hostile they can get when they want to!"

"Come off it, Andi," Justin flung out in a stage whisper. "Who do you think you're kidding? You got them here for you, not me. Look," he said, feigning weariness at her attitude. "I've had a rough day. This is silly. You wanted me to come; I'm here. Let's not keep the press waiting any longer."

Before Andi could reply, he pulled her by her arm—the same way she had guided him earlier—down the hall and into the party. Shaking free of him as soon as they reached the threshold, Andi shot across the room to a cluster of her own employees.

He began to mingle with a drive he didn't know he had, determined not to let her see him sulking or shying away from the attention. He saw her seek him out in the crowd, then glance quickly away as she seemed to work on the composure she had lost before he'd even walked in.

So much for her swooning, he thought with disdain as he waited for her to signal him that it was time for the press conference.

Reminding herself of the reason for this party, Andi decided it was time to get the announcement over with. Catching Justin's eyes again, she started to gesture for him to come to her but thought better of it, and made her way to his side instead. His eyes anticipated her through the crowd, the thick webbing of black lashes hooding them with a maddening arrogance. Chagrined, she realized as she approached him that she had never seen him dressed in evening attire, and the sight of the lean lines of his coat and the ruffled contrast of the white shirt against his skin made her wish she hadn't seen him that way now. But she would die before letting him know it looked good on him.

Their eyes locked intimately when she was face-to-face with him, each acknowledging the temporary standoff that would have to serve as a truce. "Shall we?" Andi asked, not quite able to feign a smile at him yet.

"Of course," he answered, setting an infuriatingly proprietary hand on her back as she called for the group's attention. His touch—which gave him the look of control, as if she were a mere puppet—infuriated her. She took a step forward to make him drop his hand.

The announcement was short and straightforward, and once it was made, Andi stepped back to allow the reporters to direct questions at the animator whom she had dubbed "the best in the field and the only one who provided exactly the right elements for Promised Land's needs."

When the obvious, expected questions had been answered, Jeanine Calaveras, a shrewd reporter for Given's television station, stepped forward. "Justin, tell us about your past relationship with Miss Sherman."

An amused half-grin broke out on his face, spreading maliciously to his eyes, and he glanced askance at Andi, who seemed undaunted. He started to answer, but Andi jumped in instead.

"We're old college friends," Andi explained with a dazzling smile. "We haven't seen each other in eight years, but we're delighted to be working together now."

The obvious way she tried to steer Justin from making a public blunder stung him.

"Justin," Jeanine tried again, rephrasing the question. "I understand that the two of you were more than just friends."

Justin shrugged and set his hand on the back of Andi's neck, the pressure of his fingers warning her into silence.

"You're quite right," he said, feeling Andi's muscles knotting with dread. Pencils began to jot wildly.

Andi's smile did not waiver, but her eyes glassed over with guarded contempt.

"Is that the real reason you chose him as your animator?" someone asked.

"Actually," Andi cut in again, determined to set the record straight, "Mr. Pierce's cartoon was one of several my staff brought to my attention. I had no idea he had animated Khaki's Krewe when I chose it, and if I had, the knowledge might very well have gone against him."

Justin swallowed back his distaste at her comment and parried it with one of his own. "Miss Sherman was afraid that the extent of our previous involvement may have kept her from maintaining the authority she's so used to. However, since I don't actually work *for* her and since our agreement clearly outlines both of our territories of control, we don't anticipate any problems with that." He could almost feel the hairs on her neck bristling.

"Can we expect this relationship to turn romantic again?" another bold reporter asked.

"Absolutely not," Andi said with amused resolution, taking a step forward to make Justin drop his hand. "There is no chance of that."

Although he had been about to offer a similar answer, the casual way with which Andi dismissed the possibility irked him. "None at all," he assured with chuckling certainty.

His laugh, as if the possibility were an absurdity, forced Andi to cast one last cutting remark. "I make it a policy never to date my staff members."

Staff member? Since there was no way to parry that one without continuing a verbal sparring match, Justin surrendered the last word to her. He silently vowed to confront her later, however, when the last word would be his.

When the questioning died down enough, Andi and Justin went their separate ways, mingling as they answered questions, most of a business nature, though an occasional additional query was cast from time to time about their past relationship. It became increasingly apparent as the night wore on that Andi's personal life was fascinating to the reporters, and they clung to the tidbits of information like British reporters to stories of Diana.

When the crowd had thinned down to just the Promised Land executives and a few straggling reporters, Andi found Justin leaning against a wall in what seemed to be intimate conversation with Jeanine Calaveras. The sight of his delighted smile and the woman's obvious attraction to him sent a wave of worry—not to mention jealousy—coursing through Andi. If he said the wrong thing to this woman, anything could happen. Stepping to his side, she touched his arm and smiled. "I'm not interrupting anything, am I?"

Justin shrugged. "Jeanine was just asking me about some rumors she'd heard about construction problems at Promised Land. I told her that you were the person to ask."

"Ask away," Andi said, knowing from experience with this reporter that she had probably manufactured the rumors herself.

"Well, I heard—"

A big hand landed on the woman's shoulder to stop her words, and Andi found herself looking into the benign features of B.W. Givens, the man who had made her life miserable since she'd begun work on Promised Land, the man she had made a point to avoid all evening. "No need to bother Miss Sherman with those little rumors, Jeanine," he said, his sagging jowls creasing with his false smile. "We got all we needed from her engineers."

The remark, designed to worry Andi, left her undaunted. "Good," she said in a saccharine voice. "That's why I wanted them here." Glancing back at the woman whose eyes were glued to Justin's, Andi cleared her throat. "I think it's been a productive evening," she said in dismissal of the reporter and her employer.

"Yes," Givens agreed with smug assurance. "Quite productive."

With a sigh, Jeanine stuffed her notebook back into her clutch purse and extended a hand to the animator. "I hope we'll have the pleasure of meeting again, Justin," she said, the familiar use of his name galling Andi.

"I'm sure we will," Justin said with a smile. His eyes followed the two out of the room, and then he took Andi by the arm and turned her to face him. "I think we have some unfinished business," he clipped, glancing at the others in the room. "What do you say we go to your office?"

Accepting the challenge in his eyes, she simply nodded and started toward the door.

Chapter Nine

Justin slammed the office door behind him when they were in Andi's office, the sound echoing like the crashing masks of civility they had been struggling to wear all evening. When Andi turned to face him, he saw that the look of undisguised anger on her face matched his own. "You've got a lot of nerve," he bit out, taking off his coat and tossing it on the sofa beside the wall. "I thought you would have learned a long time ago that I don't intend to kowtow for anyone, especially you."

"What are you talking about?"

"I'm talking about you on your little pedestal, making me out to be the grantee of your good graces. A lowly staff member." With a flip of his wrist, he tossed the tie on top of his coat.

"As usual, Justin," Andi said, planting her fists on her hips, "you are blowing things way out of proportion. I never called you my subordinate because I know better than to puncture that outrageous ego of yours."

A sarcastic laugh cut from Justin's throat. "You think it's my ego that's outrageous? You're the one who can't abide the fact that I've agreed to work *with* you, not *for* you."

"Your acceptance of my offer gives me some rights where you're concerned, Justin. Like it or not, it's a trade-off."

"Fine," Justin said stridently, stepping toward her. "Then let's just make it a little clearer what it is we're trading off. As far as I remember, there was nothing in our agreement about my becoming your doormat . . ."

"Where are you getting this stuff?" she threw back. "What did I say in that press conference that sounded like you were a doormat?"

"The stuff about your not dating staff members. Come on, Andi. Number one, we're each fifty percent partners in Pierce Productions, so I'm not a staff member, and number two, who asked you to date me anyway?"

"The press asked," she said, her face reddening. "They were trying to latch onto a new romance that would have wound up in the tabloids by tomorrow morning. You fed it, Justin, and you know you did. And you did it out of spite, to show me that you couldn't be harnessed!"

He knew that was true, but he didn't want to admit it. He turned away with his hands on his hips and strode to the big window of her office. How did this always happen between them? Why did he act like a child with her? Like an angry little boy bent on proving something? He turned back to her.

"You're right," he said. "I shouldn't have fed the rumor mill. I guess I just wanted to see you squirm."

"At what cost?" she asked, stepping toward him. "You'd deliberately try to make me look stupid in front of the media just so you could feel more important? Lines have to be drawn, Justin. This isn't like old times. If we're going to be working together, you need to keep your hands to yourself. The familiarity you demonstrated out there was false, and even worse, it was inappropriate. My reputation is important. People want to find something about my life that isn't right, so they can say that Promised Land is just a scam that preys on families' sense of morality. They can't believe the Shermans could really be devoted to spreading the gospel.

They want to shake it all down, Justin. I get it from every angle, every single day. Why do I have to get it from you, too?"

She could see from his face that he hadn't meant to be that to her. His face twisted as he looked down at her, and she saw the honesty, the reality, in his eyes. "I'm sorry," he whispered. "I really didn't mean to contribute to that. There's just something about you that ... rubs me the wrong way."

She swallowed the emotion in her throat and looked quickly away.

"No, that's not what I meant," he said. He reached out to touch her reassuringly, but remembering her words, he stopped himself and dropped his hand to his side. "I just meant ... well, tonight, when I got off the elevator and saw that icy rage in your eyes, it was like all my reason flicked off, and the barriers came up." He closed his eyes, and shook his head slowly. "My pride is gonna really get me one day."

When his eyes opened again, she was gazing up at him with eyes sadder than he'd ever seen. "So we're both eaten up with pride. What else is new? We knew that eight years ago."

"Yeah, I guess we did."

"Is it going to ruin us this time?" she asked. "Is it going to keep us from having any harmony ... or peace?"

"I hope not," he whispered.

They stared at each other for a long, volatile moment. Justin felt a stronger desire to kiss her than he remembered ever feeling before. If he could just brush his lips across hers one more time, to convince himself that she didn't move him like she once did, that their love had died, that it didn't have to keep stalking him like something from which he could not escape.

But she had drawn the boundaries, and he supposed he deserved them—needed them. No touches. No familiarity. No hope.

Still, as his sad gaze swept across hers, he found himself being swept on a raging rush of memory. He had loved her. And he had loved her love for him. There had been nothing like it since.

Frightened of that realization, he dropped his head. "You win, Andi." His voice was rough, hoarse, tremulous with alarming emotion.

"I don't win, Justin," she whispered. "We both lose. Neither of us can win when we're together."

The sorrow in her words made him hate himself. "If I've made that true, I'm so sorry. I might not see you as such a threat if the memories weren't so ..." His voice faltered, and he caught himself, sighing with resignation. He raised both hands and raked them roughly through his hair, closing his eyes with frustration and self-recrimination. "I'll try not to let it invade our business relationship."

Her eyes changed, grew harder, and for a moment, he wondered if, once again, he'd said the wrong thing. "That's all I ever asked of you," Andi said, her voice hard and controlled. "As a couple, we're a nightmare. But as business partners, we can do a lot together."

She moved to the door as if to dismiss him. "I think we've said enough for tonight," she stated coldly. "Tomorrow we can start fresh. And we'll work together as if we were friends. I'll work on my temper."

"And I'll work on mine," he agreed quietly. Without waiting for her reaction, he gathered his coat and left her standing there, cold, beautiful, and inconceivably alone.

Just the way he felt.

Chapter Ten

Blowing a wisp of hair out of her face, Andi watched the ice cubes bob in her Coke and pushed her untouched lunch tray away from her. Absently, she glanced up at the men sitting with her, deep in discussion about when the lake should be filled and the first test run launched for the whales in the Jonah ride. For the past three days she had been supervising the artistic development of the underwater city, making absolutely certain that no details were forgotten or neglected from laziness. Although she had people to oversee each project, she could never resist being there herself when it neared completion. She had learned long ago that there was no substitute for hands-on participation.

Besides, that niggling voice inside her head taunted, she'd do just about anything to stay out of that office while Justin and his people were settling in. The activity on the sixteenth floor, the one she had given to Pierce Productions, had been nonstop for over a week. He was hiring new people and buying new equipment, yet the work on the cartoons continued around the clock. She had been waiting for the chaos to settle before she approached him to start working with her on the park. Unfortunately, she hadn't yet seen a lull in the commotion. Whether she liked it or not, they would have to get down to business soon.

She dreaded their inevitable encounters. Since the night of the press party, Justin had avoided her as much as possible. And, she admitted ruefully, she had been avoiding him—against her better judgment, since her attempts to stay away from him were delaying some of the work on her park.

For heaven's sake, she thought, setting her glass down too roughly. She was letting her authority slip because even the thought of him intimidated her. The realization infuriated her, for she had never let anyone undermine her position before, and it had taken her a long time to earn respect as the one at the helm of Promised Land.

"Have you read this, Andi?" a construction worker asked, cutting into her thoughts. Looking up, she saw that he brandished a newspaper that bore a bird's-eye photograph of Promised Land on page one.

"No," Andi said with a moan. The articles that had come out since the press party, elaborating more on her past relationship with Justin Pierce than with his present relationship to Promised Land, had given her a new distaste for the media. Wincing, she said, "Read me the headlines."

With an amused half smile, the young man leaned back. "Electrical Problems in Promised Land Water Rides."

"You've got to be kidding," she said wearily. "Let me see that."

The man handed her the paper, and she set it on the table so the two men on either side of her could read with her. The article hinted at possible problems in the wiring and suggested that several accidents had occurred in test runs as a result of the malfunctions. "Wonderful," Andi said in a dull monotone. "The next thing you know they'll be labeling our whales electrocution chambers."

"You think some of the building inspectors are behind this?" the contractor next to her asked.

"Of course they are. They can't find anything wrong so they make it up. I'd revoke my offer to let them in if I thought it wouldn't be read as an admission of guilt."

With muttered remarks and whispered expletives at specific inspectors with whom they had collided at one point or another, the contractors cleaned their places and went back to work. Picking up the paper, Andi wondered if she should call another press conference to answer the allegations. No, she thought. It was too soon for that. Press Day, the preview day she had planned for media people from all over the country, was not that far away. If she could wait until then, she could let the park speak for itself.

Givens was obviously responsible for this. He owned the newspaper, a television station, a bank, and most of the town's other larger businesses, as well as the mayor, the city council, and various officials who had tried to make her life miserable. He had tried to own her too, she thought with a wry smirk. Thinking she'd be an easy target because of her youth and gender, he had approached her with a heavy-handed offer of "protection" at what he considered a reasonable price. When she had added threats of her own to her refusal to comply with his extortion attempts—threats of exposing him nationally as well as locally for his tactics—he had seemed to back down. She wondered now if that was just an illusion.

Her reverie was broken when the woman she had met at Justin's house the other night pulled out the chair next to her. "Thank goodness for a familiar face," she said, plopping down. "It's kind of weird walking around here with all these people I don't know. Guess it'll get worse, huh?"

Slightly taken aback by the familiarity, Andi struggled to remember her name. "I'm sorry ... I know I met you at Justin's the other night, but ... what was your name?"

"Madeline," she said. "Still is."

"Oh, that's right. And you're on Justin's staff."

"That's right. You should have stayed and had pizza with us the other night. It was great. A sweep-the-kitchen. Had everything on it. Even anchovies." She leaned forward conspiratorially and lowered her voice. "Listen, don't hold what happened the other night against Justin. He really couldn't help it."

Andi stared at her for a moment as every muscle in her body grew tense. "What night are you talking about?"

"The reception. You know, when he was late? It was kind of my fault he was late. Well, at least partially . . ."

Andi hadn't yet heard an explanation for why he was late, and now she wondered if she even wanted to know. If it had something to do with Madeline . . .

"Look, all I'm saying is don't be mad at the guy. He's trying his hardest, in spite of the fact that it's a little weird what with your history and all."

A flicker of anger flashed like lightning through her mind, but she tempered her voice. "I appreciate your concern. If you'll excuse me . . ." She got up and turned to leave but ran smack into Justin.

Frustration blended with the rage in her eyes, and she stepped back, glaring up into his face.

"Are you and Madeline getting to know each other?" he asked, casting his friend a worried glance.

Refusing to satisfy him with an answer, Andi pushed past Justin and started out of the little restaurant, feeling the heat of the sun warming her outside as she seethed within. Before she could get very far, Justin caught up with her. "What are you so mad about?"

"You!" she said. "I don't want you talking about me to your employees. About our history and how 'weird' it is to be working here. I try to maintain a certain authority over the employees here, and it's hard to do when people are gossiping about my old flame."

He let out a Herculean sigh. "I think Madeline drinks phenobarbital for breakfast. She spills out everything she knows all the rest of the day. But she means well."

Andi held her ground. "I'd appreciate it if you'd not talk about me from now on. I don't like people knowing about my personal life."

"They're my friends, okay? I share my life with them, and all my frustrations. They know I used to be close to you, and they know how it went wrong. I can't take it back, and if I could, I wouldn't. So get over it. As a matter of fact, you might try making a few friends of your own."

The comment made her even more furious. Without another word, she went to her electric car and drove rapidly out of his sight.

Chapter Eleven

Justin stewed in his office, slamming things down and kicking chairs, when Madeline came ambling in. "Hey, boss. What's ruffled your feathers?"

"Andi Sherman," he said. "And you! Where do you get off talking to her like you did today?"

Madeline looked genuinely surprised. "Talking to her how? I was trying to make friends."

Justin raked a hand through his hair. "Look, from now on, if you talk to her, don't mention me at all. Okay? In fact, just stay away from her entirely."

"Well, how am I gonna do that? We work in the same—"

The door flew open, and Gene came running in, breathless. "Justin! It's ABC television on the phone."

Justin's eyebrows arched, and he looked from Gene to Madeline, who had suddenly sprung to attention. "What do they want?"

"I don't know!" Gene said. "But we sent them a tape, remember? Our proposal for the Saturday morning spot? Answer it, Justin!"

Justin looked down at the phone, then back at both of them. "All right, everybody out. I'll let you know what it's about when I get off the phone."

Madeline and Gene both groaned as they left the office, closing the door behind them.

Outside Justin's office, Madeline pressed her ear against the door, and Gene, B.J., Nathan, and the others all gathered behind her.

"What's he saying? Can you hear anything?"

"No, nothing. Shhh. He's talking!"

Dead silence as everyone waited.

"I can't hear what he's saying!" Madeline said. "This isn't fair. Get me a glass. I've seen it work on *Lucy*."

B.J. scrambled to find her a glass, but only came up with a dirty coffee mug. She pressed it against the door and tried again.

"Anything?" Gene asked.

"Nothing," she said. "Why won't he talk louder?"

Suddenly the door was opened, and Madeline and the rest of them fell in. Justin jumped back and looked down at them with a grin. "May I help you?"

Madeline waited until everyone was off of her before she could pull herself to her feet. The coffee mug was still in her hand. "Uh ... I just ... was waiting to see if you wanted some coffee."

He glanced into the dirty cup. "In that?"

She forgot about the cup and looked up at him. "Oh, Justin! Quit keeping us in suspense. What did they want?"

"Oh, nothing," he said, checking a hangnail on his thumb. "They've just decided ... *to give Khaki's Krewe a half-hour on the Saturday morning line-up!*"

Madeline screamed, and the others began yelling with glee, jumping up and down, hugging each other, patting each other on the backs so hard that they almost knocked each other over.

"We're going to New York," Justin said. "We have to have a meeting with the ABC execs and sign all the papers. Gene and Nathan are going with me."

"All right!" Gene shouted, and Nathan punched at the air.

"Not fair!" Madeline said. "Why can't I go?"

"I need you and B.J. here," Justin said. "We're going to have to double up on work to do all we have to do to get the characters ready for Promised Land, and still make deadlines for ABC. We're going to have to have twice the staff we planned, but that's no problem. Between Promised Land and ABC, we can hire as many as we want."

Madeline screamed again, and the others joined her in delighted whoops.

The smell of soap and shampoo-laced steam drifted into her office from the adjoining bathroom, and Andi opened a window to let it air out. She rarely used that shower, for she couldn't stand having her work sanctuary filled with humidity, but today had been an exception. The Louisiana heat had been stronger than usual for April, and she had worked with a vengeance to escape her pain over her most recent confrontation with Justin. When she'd come back to the office to face the paperwork that had piled up in her absence, she had decided not to take the time to go home and shower.

The phone rang as she unrolled one of the blueprints on her desk, and tossing a damp strand of hair over her shoulder, she answered.

"Look outside that window and tell me what you see." Georgia Sherman's voice sounded tired.

Andi did as ordered. "Just the sunset, Mom," she said, stifling a yawn.

"Exactly. And, although you might not know it by past experience, that usually means quitting time."

Andi smiled. "Where are you?"

"At the hospital," Georgia said, and Andi could tell from her tone that she was depressed. "I've decided that we both need to get out. I'm taking you to dinner."

"Mom, I really don't—" she began, but cut herself off as she realized that her mother might need this. "I really don't feel like getting dressed up. I'm too tired. If I can go in what I'm wearing, you're on."

"Fine," she agreed. "I'll pick you up in about an hour."

Hanging up the phone, Andi pulled herself out of her chair and went to the window, leaning into the sill at her waist while she tried to absorb the serenity of the sunset. What would life be like a year from now, she wondered, with her park open and full of ecstatic children and adults, with perhaps her father recovered and enjoying the success his daughter had maintained during his illness, and, of course, with Justin contributing to and sharing in that success? Would she still feel as alone as she did now, or would the whirling emotions have settled by then, making her Justin's friend and partner rather than his arch rival?

She closed her eyes as the wind blew through her hair, and breathed a silent prayer for God's help in lifting her sagging spirits.

Justin knocked on her office door, and heard the low, "Come in."

He opened the door and stepped into the broken rectangle of light cast by the setting sun. He closed the door behind him and squinted as he found her silhouetted against the window, obstructing his view of her face. The heady scent of her shower steam lingered in the room, and he breathed it in.

"I thought you would have gone home by now," Andi said, her voice low as she crossed her arms guardedly and walked toward him. When she became more than an opaque shadow, he saw that she had changed clothes and showered since morning, and her hair shimmered like long threads of silk.

"Not me," he said, sinking to the couch instead of the chair in front of her desk. "I'm not one to knock off just because the sun goes down."

"No," Andi said, leaning against the outer edge of her desk. "I knew you wouldn't be."

Justin crossed his legs and let his eyes peruse the brown blouse that made her hair seem lighter, the off-white jeans that accented her small frame.

"So, what brings you here?" she asked with a speculative gleam in her eyes.

He shrugged and set his chin on his thumb, stroking his chiseled jaw with a finger. "Have you eaten yet?"

Andi narrowed her eyes and stared at him for a moment, trying to decide if he was asking her to dinner or simply making a polite inquiry. His ambiguity set her on guard, and she dared not make assumptions. "No, not yet. Why?"

"I thought maybe we could go out for a bite and talk."

Andi's heart lurched. Was he making a move toward ending their enmity? Even after their recent explosive encounters? Could it be possible that some inner stirring was plaguing him too? She opened her mouth to say yes, until she remembered the plans she had just made with her mother. She blew out a deflated sigh. "I can't tonight. I have other plans. I'm going to—"

"Forget it," he cut in. "It was business anyway. We can talk about it here just as easily."

The casual way he dispelled the notion that he was asking her for a date set her defenses up another notch. "Fine," she said, walking around her desk to sit down. "I've got about an hour. Start talking."

Leaning forward and planting his elbows on his knees, he looked at the floor, then brought his eyes back to her. "I had a call from ABC today," he said, his voice deliberately matter-of-fact. "They want to give Khaki's Krewe a spot on their Saturday morning lineup."

Andi caught her breath, momentarily forgetting her anger. "Oh, Justin. That's wonderful!"

A half smirk tipped his lips as he carefully harnessed his own enthusiasm. "What? No explosions? No lectures about conflicts of interest?"

Andi's excitement began to ebb as she realized he was looking for a fight. "It's not a conflict, Justin. We discussed this before I bought into your company." Studying his expressionless eyes, she frowned again. "Aren't you happy about it?"

"Of course I am," he said mildly, sitting back and stretching an arm across the back of the sofa. "It's been a goal of mine for years, and it's still one of my highest priorities."

"Above Promised Land?" she asked, though she already knew the answer.

He shrugged. "I wanted this before there *was* a Promised Land."

Andi bit her lip and tapped her fingertips together, realizing that if the offer had come two weeks earlier, the merger might never have taken place. "It'll be okay, Justin. I'm happy for you, and I can live with it."

His mouth crooked in a slight smile. "Good."

Setting her chin on the heel of her hand, Andi grinned and studied the handsome figure slouched with indolent grace on her sofa. "You must be feeling pretty proud of yourself right about now."

Justin shrugged, his blue eyes focusing on the ceiling, glimmering with something close to worry. "I'm not getting worked up yet. They want changes in the story lines, want me to tone down the Christian theme a bit. They also want the humor to be less subtle. They don't credit kids with enough intelligence to know when to laugh. I'll have to see how flexible they are before I'll sign anything. We'll see how it goes when I get there."

"Get where?"

"New York. They want me to fly up there to finalize things."

She looked at him for a moment as the business side of her began to usurp the part of her that enjoyed Justin's success. "Not anytime soon, I hope."

"I've made arrangements to leave the day after tomorrow."

"You've what?" Andi snapped, leaning forward, her fingers clamping on her chair's arms. "Didn't it occur to you to check with me first?"

"Not for a minute," he said, his tight voice laced with satisfaction.

Andi pulled out of her chair and leaned on her desk. "Justin, I own half of Pierce Productions!"

"I run it," he pronounced sharply, "and I don't plan to ask your permission every time I make a decision. I came here to fill you in."

"Then let me fill *you* in. You can't go traipsing off to New York! Promised Land needs you right now!"

"I thought you just said you were happy for me. That you could live with it."

"Well, I didn't think it meant you'd completely neglect your responsibility to Promised Land! We have an enormous amount of work to get done in the next few weeks."

He sprang up. "Well, you're just going to have to wait! Good grief, Andi. I'll just be gone a couple of days. It's not like I took your money and skipped the country. It'll be good for Promised Land in the long run. The more exposure my cartoons get, the more people will want to visit the park. That was the whole idea when we started this thing."

Andi tried to swallow back her temper and looked down at her desk. Was she angry because he was abandoning the park—or because he was abandoning her? She hoped her reaction wasn't merely personal.

It wasn't, she told herself. She really did need him here.

She turned to him. "Can't you send someone else? We need you to help us with the automated figures of your characters. And we're in the middle of planning the ad campaign."

"I'm taking Gene and Nathan with me, but they can't speak for me. Madeline can help you with the robots. She knows the characters as well as anybody."

Her eyes flashed back to his. With teeth clenched, she said, "Madeline is not the president of Pierce Productions! You are! You'll just have to put it off."

"I won't," he bit out, his blue eyes unwavering. They stared at each other for a moment, caught in a battle of wills so strong that each would have sacrificed the cause for a moment of victory. "Have you forgotten what the terms of our agreement were?" he grated. "Doesn't the fact that I still own half of my company mean anything to you?" Before she could respond, he leaned toward her, the disquieting strength in his body visibly constrained as he extended a finger emphasizing his point. "I'm not going to stand here and let you dictate where I go and what I do. If you want a fight, Andi, you'll get one!"

Andi's back was ramrod straight, belying the fact that inwardly she was wilting with the lack of an argument. She opened her mouth to formulate one anyway, when the telephone shrilled out, adding the perfect touch to the shouting match they had found themselves embroiled in. Snatching it out of its cradle, she shouted, "Hello!"

Justin's heart was still pounding with the force of his rage, but his breathing slowed when he saw the blood drain from Andi's face. Her hand came up to cover her mouth and her green eyes misted over with a frightening mixture of fear and pain.

"What happened?" she whispered into the phone. Her hand went up to clutch the roots of her hair and she nodded, wetting her quivering lips. "I'll ... I'll be right there." She tried to hang up the phone, but her hand was trembling so badly that she couldn't.

Justin took the phone from her hand and set it in its cradle. Taking her by the shoulders, he turned her toward him with a sudden surge of gentleness. "What is it?"

Her eyes were glassy with chaotic emotions and tears that would not spill. "It's ... my dad ... he's had ... a heart attack ..."

He took a step toward her as if to hold her, but stopped himself. "He's not ... I mean, he's still alive, isn't he?"

"Yes!" she blurted, then caught her breath in a sob. "I think so. They wouldn't say." She covered her face as the possibilities took hold of her. Then she lifted her head and looked up into eyes that shared her pain and offered to help her shoulder the burden. "I have to get to him. He needs me. Mom needs me."

"I'll take you," Justin whispered. A sob racked her, and she pressed her palm to her mouth, as if failing to hold back her emotion would mean failing her father somehow.

The intensity of the restrained grief and fear in her eyes broke his heart. He couldn't remember ever having seen such vulnerability seep through her strong constitution before.

"I thought he was going to wake up," she whispered. "I thought he'd come out of it one day, and see what I'd done with Promised Land, and—"

In that moment, Justin abandoned his agreement not to touch her. This wasn't business, and Andi needed to be held. "Shhh," he whispered, pulling her into his arms. "It'll be all right. Everything'll be fine."

Her arms tightened around his waist as her tears soaked straight through to his heart. In that instant, he thought he would do anything in his power to spare her another moment of pain.

Chapter Twelve

The sterile hospital smell invaded even the elevator, making the reality of pain and dying more immediate, more of a monster from which Justin yearned to protect Andi.

Her tears had dried, and as the elevator made its ascent, she held her head in stubborn defiance of the most likely possibility. "He'll be all right," she said with that desperate bravado he had heard in her before. "I'm sure of it. By now he's fine."

Justin prayed for her sake that she was right. More than anything, he wanted to take her home where he could shield her from this place. Whatever the outcome, he decided, he would be there for her.

When the elevator door opened, he felt Andi bracing herself with a deep breath that seemed to harden her muscles. Slowly, the two stepped onto the floor and started up the corridor leading to her father's room, but the sight of her mother in a lobby chair, her hands covering her face, stopped them.

"M-Mom," Andi stuttered in a hoarse, broken voice.

Her mother looked up at them. "Honey." Her pale, drawn face looked at least fifteen years older than it had just yesterday. Her eyes were bloodshot and red-rimmed, and standing seemed to take all the energy she still contained. She smiled wanly at Justin. "It's good to see you again, Justin," she said quietly. Then, taking Andi's shoulders, she forced her to look at her. "We lost him," she said in a racked voice, as if the end would not come until the words were spoken.

"No!" The word came out in an angry cry, Andi's head shaking wildly to parry the words. "He'll be okay. He . . ." She looked at her mother, then fell into her arms. "Oh, Mom!"

"He's been gone a long time, honey," her mother said softly, rocking her gently back and forth and touching her hair, as her own tears traveled down her face. "We were the ones who were hanging on. We have to let go now."

"No!" Andi cried. "He might have come to. He might have lived!"

"But he didn't," her mother said in a wooden voice.

Justin watched, helpless, as Andi tried to pull the crumbling pieces of herself back together. At any moment, he thought, the thin filament of her control would snap completely. Taking a deep breath, she stepped away from her mother. "I have to see him," she said.

"You can't, honey. He's not in his room anymore."

Andi lost whatever strength she still harbored. "No!" she cried, dropping her hands to her sides in helpless abandonment. "I never said good-bye."

Her mother closed her arms around Andi's frail body, her own tears wetting Andi's shirt as she quaked against her. Then she stepped back and offered her to Justin. "Take her home," her mother said quietly. "And don't leave her alone. I'll stay and take care of the . . . the arrangements."

The word immediately brought Andi erect and rigid. "No," she said flatly. "I'll help. He's my father."

"And he was my husband," her mother countered, her adamant eyes making Andi back down. "He was my best friend. I insist, honey. I want to."

Andi nodded dumbly. Looking small and helpless, she turned to Justin. Gently, he took her arm and wrapped it through his. "I'll take care of her, Mrs. Sherman," Justin promised.

Andi's mother nodded, her eyes bright with tears.

"I know you will, Justin," she said quietly.

Justin had considered taking her to his house. Instead, he took her to her own home and made up his mind to stay no matter how strong she pretended to be. He tried to tell himself that she needed him, but in his heart he didn't know if the need he felt was hers or his. There was something about her now, something soft and sweet, something too close to the woman he remembered, the one who had plagued his memories for eight long years.

Andi's apartment was not what he expected. He had prepared himself for plush white carpeting, velvet upholstered furniture, elaborate chandeliers. Instead he found a room with bare parquet floors and red throw rugs, bright red printed furniture with black tables, and Oriental prints on the walls. The simplicity of the apartment sent a warm surge through him as he led her in.

When he had set her on the sofa and gotten her a glass of tea, he lowered himself next to her and watched her sip it. He sensed that false bravado seeping back into her shoulders as she lifted her chin, and he knew what was coming.

"I appreciate your taking me to the hospital, Justin," she said softly. "And helping me home. I'm all right now, though, and ..." Tears sprang to her eyes again and she choked them back. "You don't have to stay. I really just need some rest and then—"

"I'm not going anywhere right now," Justin declared softly, leaning back on the couch and pulling her with him. "If you want me to, I'll call your date and tell him what happened."

"My date?" She wiped at her eyes and gave him a puzzled look. "Oh, you mean for dinner. There's no need. It was my mother."

Unaccountable relief surged through him that there wasn't some other man in the wings who had more right to comfort her than he. With great gentleness he pulled her head against his chest.

"Really," she tried again, forcing her voice to stop quivering. "I'd rather be alone. It was a shock at first and I kind of fell apart, but I'm okay now."

"I'm staying," he said again, his deep baritone vibrating against her face.

His persistence seemed to shake her, and she pulled out of his arms and stood up. Going to the fireplace, she leaned against the black mantel. "Justin, please. I really want to be alone."

"The last thing you need tonight is to be alone," he said as if it was a fundamental fact that could not be argued.

Something about his stubborn insistence seemed to rankle her. "Being alone is something I'm quite familiar with," she bit out. "I prefer it. Especially right now. Please."

"I'm not leaving," he said, rising quietly and facing her off with his hands hung at his sides.

"Why?" The word came out as an exasperated cry that reached the dusty chambers of his heart. "You hated my father!"

He didn't answer for a long time, for he wasn't certain why himself. Was it because he knew that if he left her now he'd never see past that icy casing again?

"But I care for you." The raw honesty in his answer left him strangely warm and bewildered, but it inscribed itself on his heart like temporary salve that would hurt worse when the comfort wore off. He stepped toward her as she turned her back to him, leaning her head into the mantel, her shoulders shaking with the intensity of her sobs. He slid his arms around her from the back, pulling her against him until she turned in his arms and clasped him around the neck, her face buried against his shoulders. "You can call me names, tell me I'm invading on a private moment, slap me and abuse me," he whispered, closing his eyes and kissing her hair. "But I won't leave you right now."

He lifted her in his arms, sat down on the couch, and held her against him for what seemed to be hours as she cried herself to exhaustion. And just before she drifted into her restless cocoon of sleep, he heard her mumble feverishly against his chest, "I miss him."

Instinctively, his arms tightened around her, and he buried his face in her hair. An enormous sense of his own loss was growing inside him, seeking out all the dark, cold corners that had lain empty since he'd left her. He knew what it was to miss someone he loved.

When her hand fell limply onto her stomach, he shifted her off of his lap. With a soft murmur, she curled up on one end of the couch and pulled her knees to her chest, a pained expression on her face. Justin gazed down at her, gently stroking back the hair over her ear until her face relaxed in distracted rest.

But it was only momentary. As soon as he lifted his fingers, the frown on her forehead clefted again. Even in her dreams, she was grieving.

Her torment made his heart ache, for he had no idea how to intrude on her dreams and order the torturous monsters of mourning to leave her. He pulled off the afghan lying over the back of her couch and covered her gently.

"Shhh. It's just me," he said, his voice reassuring her with tenderness he didn't know he had. And as if the words were all she needed to defy the shadows taunting her mind, he watched her relax and resume her sleep.

The emotion coursing through him alarmed him. *Neither of us can win when we're together.* The words stabbed his heart as he realized he had gone to great lengths to convince her of that. His foolish pride, always at battle with hers, turned all his victories into self-defeats.

But he had forgotten how strong his love for her had been.

Frightened by the strength of those feelings renewing themselves in his heart, he slipped out of her apartment and raced home, where he knew he could isolate himself from the kind of pain that came with loving someone that deeply.

Andi's eyelashes fluttered, then closed again. A strange feeling of security enveloped her, and she opened them again, struggling to orient herself.

She had fallen asleep on the couch, in Justin's arms. He had covered her up with an afghan, but now he was gone. Had her stupid vulnerability frightened him away? Her neediness? Her weakness?

She sat up, and suddenly she remembered why she had cried so much in his arms, why she had fallen asleep the way she had . . .

Her father was dead . . .

She raced to the phone, dialed her mother's number, but got a busy signal. She had to get over there, she thought. She had to help her. There was so much to do.

She went to the door, intent on hurrying out, but Justin was just getting off the elevator, his eyes tired and his face covered with stubble. He had never looked better.

"Justin!"

He brandished the bags that smelled of coffee and Egg McMuffins. "I thought I'd bring you breakfast. Where were you going?"

"To my mother's," she said. "I have to help her. I have to—"

"I've already spoken to your mother, Andi. She called me a little while ago. She said that most of the details of the funeral were taken care of months ago. She said she had been awake most of the night, but thought she could sleep now. She was going to take the phone off the hook. She's okay, Andi."

Andi wilted back from the door, and suddenly realized how bad she must look. Her hair had not been brushed, and her eyes were swollen . . .

Justin came in and closed the door behind him.

"Thank you for . . . what you did last night, Justin. Bringing me home, listening, putting up with me."

"I wouldn't have done it if I hadn't wanted to."

"But you have to get ready for your trip to New York."

"I'm not going. At least, not when I planned. I'm staying until after the funeral."

She didn't even try to hide the gratitude in her eyes. And he didn't try to hide the emotions coursing through his. He gazed down at her, his eyes eloqent with unspoken words that she couldn't interpret. She had been wrong when she'd told him neither of them could win, she thought as her heart ached for his touch. Right now, he was letting her be the winner, sacrificing whatever victory of his own he might have found in New York.

Maybe it wasn't about winning, she thought. Maybe that wasn't the most important thing to him anymore.

"What would I have done without you last night?" she asked.

"What you always do, Andi. You would have been fine. You would have pulled together, and taken over the funeral arrangements, and made sure everything was done just right."

She sighed. "That's probably what I should have done."

"No," he said. "Your mother wanted to do it. He was her husband. It seemed important to her. Maybe it was her way of saying good-bye to him."

She thought that over for a moment. She had never been good at good-byes. It was her downfall. Did Justin know how she had grieved over their good-bye? Had he grieved for her?

She had to know if what she'd seen in his eyes, felt in his attention, was something real, or something that had evolved out of tragedy. Was it sympathy? Just kindness to help her through a rough time?

As she followed him quietly into the kitchen, she realized that her father had once come between them. Now, through the grace of God, he was the means by which they were being brought together.

Justin postponed his trip to New York and stayed by Andi's side for the next three days as she fulfilled the mechanical obligations of being her father's only daughter. Distant relatives, friends, and acquaintances trickled in from all over the country for what was fast becoming a press event. Because he had lain unconscious for so long prior to his death, few of the "mourners" were sensitized to Andi's and her mother's suffering. No one looked past the smile on her face or the numb expression in her eyes, and talk was much the same as it would have been at a family reunion.

But later when he was alone with her, Justin saw those ice walls melt as she leaned on him as she had never leaned on anyone before. Together, they had long earnest discussions on how to best handle the business during this time. And together they devised a strategy for dealing with the press, which had descended on them like vultures.

It was becoming common conjecture that Promised Land would inevitably fail without the Andrew Sherman name behind it. His daughter had carried it off thus far, the pundits agreed, but the real test would come when the park opened. From where would the quality and perfection that was evidenced in his toy and computer products come? Just how strong was his daughter's glacial constitution?

Justin himself was impressed by her strength. He marveled at the way she seemed to stand on her own when they were in public, as if nothing had changed, convincing everyone that business would continue as usual after the funeral. He learned a new appreciation for her ability to be competent and human at the same time, but in the back of his mind he harbored the needling doubt that what she shared with him was anything more than desperation borne of deep loneliness. Their no-touch rule had been breached only briefly, and now, as she regained control of her emotions, he waited for her to give him some sign that the familiarity would not be inappropriate. The last thing he wanted was to take advantage of her now. But each time their eyes met across the room or their arms brushed in public, he sensed her longing for more, the same thing he longed for, something more than business or friendship.

Moment by moment Andi seemed to draw on the strength that he offered freely, with silent smiles and quiet gestures. But he tried his hardest to avoid touching her, or conveying his feelings in words. Not yet. Not until the crisis had passed. Then he would see what remained.

Two days after the funeral, Andi went back to work. Using business as an excuse to see Justin, she went to the sixteenth floor, through the hallways flanked by cavernous rooms full of inkers, painters, in-betweeners, and paint checkers. Other rooms occupied by camera operators, film editors, and Xerox operators led to the spacious offices of the master animators, all within easy access of Justin's plush office.

Making her way through boxes and misplaced furniture outside his office, Andi saw that Justin's door was partially opened. Raising her fist to knock on the jamb, she heard the sound of voices and hesitated.

"I know it doesn't make sense to you, Madeline," Justin was saying. "But I do have an obligation to her."

"Obligation? Justin, the merger had nothing to do with this kind of obligation. When are you going to snap out of it and realize that the funeral is over and now it's time to move on? Don't get me wrong, Justin. My heart goes out to her and all, but I don't want you ruining everything we've built together for some overblown sense of obligation."

Andi took a few steps back, letting the words sink in. Obligation? They were obviously talking about her. Was that all the past few days had been? *Obligation?*

The words shot like a poisonous arrow through Andi's heart, and she turned and fled through the labyrinth of bustling activity, trying desperately to maintain her dignity, telling herself that it didn't matter, that she did not love him, that she had to prove her strength to him, so he wouldn't see her as some broken, pathetic thing to whom he owed something.

Determined to bury herself in her work, she spent the next few hours catching up on paperwork that required absolute concentration. But when Justin knocked on her door later and came in before she answered, the mental walls blocking thought and pain shattered, and she went rigid, inwardly groping for control. She refused to meet his warm smile with one of her own. Busying herself with papers, she asked, "What is it, Justin? I'm really busy."

Her words were met with dead silence. She looked up, keeping her eyes cold and distant. For a moment he stared at her. "Well, I wanted to talk to you about my trip to New York," he said uncertainly. "I've been putting it off—"

"You should go as soon as possible."

He hesitated again, and his face began to redden. "Is something wrong?"

"No. What could be wrong?"

"I don't know."

"I'm just busy," she said. "I have a lot of things to catch up on."

He sat down and leaned his elbows on his knees. "Okay." If she wanted things all business, he could make them all business. "I've decided to leave B.J. in charge instead of Madeline. He can answer for me on just about anything."

Andi stiffened in her chair and picked up her pencil again, tapping the eraser on her desk as she feigned interest in the report in front of her. "Did you decide Madeline couldn't handle it?"

His eyes narrowed. "No. I've decided to take her with me."

Andi's eyes came up to his in a flash, and she fought the alarms ringing through her mind. Was that why Madeline was so worried about his *obligation?* Was Justin involved with her? She blinked back the mist threatening her eyes, refusing to let him see what this was costing her. "I see," was all she trusted herself to say.

From his studied appraisal of her coolness, she could see that he was completely baffled by her attitude. Did he think she'd fallen so deeply in love that she was blind? "She's going to be looking for new animators while she's there," he volunteered.

"You don't have to explain to me, Justin," Andi bit out through lips tight with rancor. "You have no ..." She stopped on the word "obligation," and rephrased it. "You don't owe me a thing."

Slow, building anger seeped into his features. "What is your problem?"

"I *told* you I have no problem," she said, glancing toward the door. "Is that all you wanted to talk to me about?"

With glowering eyes, he stared at her across the desk, giving no indication that he would move. "There were other things," he said in a wooden voice. "But they don't seem important anymore."

"Fine," Andi said, anxious for him to leave before she imploded. "Then I hope the two of you have a wonderful trip."

"There are four of us going."

"Oh, yes," Andi said, trying to ignore the disbelief glimmering in his narrowed eyes. "Gene and Nathan. I hope you all have a wonderful trip."

With deep lines of indignation and battlement etching his face, Justin turned and strode to the door, then pivoted back to her, a look of chilling disgust coloring his eyes. "Bet on it," he said, and then he slammed out of her office.

Andi wasn't certain how long she stared at the door. With fists clenched, she ordered her mind to numb her senses, but pain pulsed through her nevertheless. Just as she started to give in to the utter despair, Justin burst back through the door.

His eyes were shooting sparks and fuming with fury, and he slammed the door behind him and went to her desk, leaning across it again. His face was inches from hers, his breath hot against her face, and she leaned back, speechless.

"I started to leave it like that," hc said in a dangerously quiet voice. "But then I thought how the last few days have at least earned me the right to an explanation. So let's hear it."

Carefully reconstructing the walls over her emotions, Andi swallowed. "I haven't been myself the last few days," she said in a hoarse, distant voice. Dropping her eyes to her hands, she went on. "I needed someone and you were there. I appreciate it, but I'm back to myself now."

A flicker of pain passed across his features. "And so you don't *need* me anymore. Is that it?"

"Yes," she said, still watching her hands.

A rough hand gripped her chin and jerked her face up to his. "Look at me when you say that, Andi. Look in my eyes and tell me that nothing's been happening between us for the last few days."

Swallowing back the tears in her throat, she reminded herself of the words Madeline had said. *I don't want you ruining everything we've built together over some overblown sense of obligation.* She wondered what, exactly, they *had* built together, and why he hadn't told her about it in the beginning. She should have seen it, she thought, when Madeline admitted that it had been her fault that Justin had been late for the reception. Maybe she was trying to tell her something more important—something Andi hadn't wanted to hear.

But it wasn't too late to salvage some of her self-respect. "It meant something at the time," she forced out. "But let's not blow it out of proportion."

"You're right," he bit out. "Let's not." Without further warning, he slammed out of her office again.

Chapter Thirteen

Andi propped her feet on her mother's marble-topped coffee table and leaned her head back on the Victorian sofa. Her mother sat next to her, her own feet propped up.

"I'm glad it's over. All those people here, trying to comfort me, bringing all that food, as if one person could possibly eat so much." She sighed. "Why do they bring food, anyway?"

"I guess they just don't know what else to do." Andi took her mother's hand and squeezed it. "You probably did need comfort, Mom. And heaven knows I wasn't a lot of help."

"I'm glad you had Justin to help you through it. I was so busy with all those people." She laughed lightly. "It was kind of nice hearing all the old stories about your father, from people I had never even met. A lot of people respected him."

The Persian cat, Sheba, jumped up on Andi's lap, and she began to pet it as she reflected on her father. "Remember the stupid things Dad would say to the cat?"

Her mother laughed. "Yes. He'd look at Sheba and say, 'So you're a kitty, huh?'"

"And he made up that silly song—"

Together, they sang, "So bad kitty ... so bad kitty ..."

They wilted together in laughter.

Her mother's amusement died on a sigh. "It's good to remember the good times, isn't it? For so long, all those memories seemed to be trapped. All I could see was how he was, lying on that bed. ..."

Andi's smile faded to sadness, and her mother hugged her. "Oh, honey, don't look so sad. He's free now. We'll see him again before we know it."

"I just miss him so much," she whispered. "I wanted so much for him to see Promised Land."

"Well, I have my regrets, too. I wish he could have had the chance to see how good Justin was to you this past week. Maybe finally give his blessings on something he should have approved years ago."

Andi stiffened slightly and leaned forward, propping her chin on her hand. "No, Mom, you've got it all wrong. There's nothing to give a blessing to. Justin and I are just friends, at best."

Her mother gave her a surprised look. "Well, now, my eyes may not be what they used to be, but what I see between the two of you is not friendship. And frankly, I thought it said quite a bit about Justin that he would support you so sweetly through all this, when he had every reason to hate Drew."

"He was sweet," Andi agreed. She wondered what he was doing now. Was he with Madeline, talking about his "obligations" to Andi? She hadn't heard from him since he left, and she knew she wouldn't. "But nothing's going to happen with Justin and me."

"Never?"

"No, Mom. Sorry."

Her mother dusted the cat hair off of her lap. "Well, I'm not going to give up that easily. If that young man has the sense he seems to, he won't either. What is it, anyway? Did you two have a fight?"

"No," Andi said, deciding she was too soul-weary to lie. "Mom, I went to his office to see him, and I heard him telling this woman he works with that he felt obligated to me, and she was trying to convince him he had no obligation. Of course, she was right. He doesn't owe me anything. But she seemed to have a vested interest. And he took her to New York with him."

Her mother caught her breath and dropped her feet. Shifting on the couch to face her, she asked, "Are you sure? Even if some other woman is in love with him, it doesn't mean he returns it. Who is this woman?"

"Someone who shares all his dreams."

"Well, so do you!"

"Yeah, but she's helping him work on his. It's different."

"All right," her mother said, trying to sort it all out. "But for the last few days, he was with you."

"But I don't want to be somebody's obligation, and I don't need anyone being with me out of pity. And if he's involved with her, then I sure don't want to be the other woman." Tears came to her eyes, and she fought them back, but her mother hugged her again.

"Oh, honey. This is awful. You don't need another heartbreak after losing your father."

Andi tried to pull herself together. "I'm okay, Mom. Really. And I shouldn't blame him. It's not his fault, really. He saw how distraught I was; what else could he have done?" Her voice trailed off, words hanging in air.

"Come to Paris with me," her mother said. "It'll be good for both of us to get away for a while."

"I can't leave now," Andi said. "You go ahead. You need a vacation, but I can't leave the park. We're too close to getting it finished, and there are too many decisions that have to be made. Plus, Givens is probably saving his best efforts for the end. He doesn't want the park to open. Really, I'm going to be so busy from here on out, that I won't even think about Justin. And he sure won't be thinking about me." Her eyes settled on some distant spot as her mind reflected on their last conversation, the one where she'd told him she didn't need him anymore.

"All right, then. Come on," her mother said, taking her hand and pulling her to her feet. "Let's go raid some of those dishes in the refrigerator. Maybe you can help me identify some of them."

Andi forced a smile and followed her mother to the kitchen.

Chapter Fourteen

Justin sat brooding at the table near the window in the restaurant at Rockefeller Center, close to the ABC building where he'd spent the afternoon. He saw Madeline come in, and the hostess led her to his table.

"Uh-oh," Madeline said when she saw him. "What happened? It fell through, didn't it?"

He tried to snap out of it and shook his head. "No. Everything's fine. Better than fine. Looks like we have a deal."

Madeline punched the air and spun around, then composed herself and sat down. "That's great, Justin! So great! So why do you have that I-lost-my-best-friend look on your face?"

He refrained from answering that it was because he'd lost his best friend. "I just have a lot on my mind. It's all kind of overwhelming."

"In a good way, though. Listen, I met some great people at the art school. Several of them are about to graduate."

"Great. Hire them."

Madeline sat back in her chair, as if surprised that it had been so easy. "Really?"

"Yeah. We're gonna need everybody we can get. I trust you to pick good people. That's why I brought you."

She frowned and leaned forward on the table. "Are you sure you're all right?"

He grinned.

"Really," she said. "What's wrong? If you don't tell me within five minutes, I'm going to climb on this table and start singing 'God Bless America' at the top of my lungs. It won't be pretty."

He rubbed his face. "Nothing. It's just a run-in I had with Andi before we left."

"A run-in? It's got you so distracted that you're completely missing one of the most significant days in your professional life, and you call it a 'run-in'?"

"All right. A fight, okay? We had a fight."

"About what?"

"About ... nothing."

Madeline started to stand and began humming "God Bless America."

"I'm telling you the truth," Justin said, grabbing her hand and forcing her back down. "Now hush."

"Don't tell me it was about nothing," Madeline said. "I don't take evasions well."

"Maybe it's none of your business."

"Maybe," Madeline said. "But that never stopped me before. I'm feeling very patriotic."

He looked back out the window. "The truth is, I don't know what it was about. She just got a bee in her bonnet and started snipping at me about how she hasn't been herself for the last few days."

"Well, she hasn't. Her father died. Who would be?"

"No, I mean ... all the time we spent together ..." He rubbed his jaw hard, then shook his head. "Never mind."

"Wait a minute. You mean she cut you loose?"

He dropped his face in his hands. He was tired. So tired. "Yeah, something like that. Told me she didn't need me anymore."

"Oh, Justin, I'm sorry."

He slid his fingers down his face and stared over his fingertips at a couple strolling past the window. "The thing is, something triggered it. Andi's moody, sure, but not that moody. And when she feels things, she feels them deep. Too deep, I used to think. But she doesn't turn hot and cold just like that."

"What do you think it was?"

"Who knows? She's sure not going to tell me."

"Well, have you tried calling her since you've been here?"

"Nope. Not going to."

"Why not?"

"The ball's in her court, Madeline. She cut the strings. I don't have to grovel to keep a woman's interest."

"No, you don't. But playing these games isn't going to help."

"Who's playing games?"

"She is. And you are." She shoved her curls back from her face. "Correct me if I'm wrong, but isn't that what happened with her the last time? You were both playing games. You both lost. You disappeared out of anger, and she got the wrong impression, and then you came back, and she was still reacting to the disappearance, and she said some things she probably didn't mean, and you said some things you probably didn't mean—"

The words shot straight to his heart, because he knew they were true. Andi had been right from the beginning. There was no winning when they were together.

"Let's just change the subject, okay?"

"All right," Madeline said.

"So where are Gene and Nathan?"

"Nathan had a date with one of the artists he met at the school. And Gene . . . well, talk about losers . . ."

Justin's eyebrows shot up. "All right, spit it out. What did Gene do?"

She looked out the window. "Nothing."

Justin grinned and began to sing "God bless America."

Madeline laughed and tried to quiet him. "All right, Justin. I'll tell you everything. But only if you'll take me out tonight. I'm tired of sitting alone in my hotel room waiting for the phone to ring."

"I can relate," he said. "Where do you want to go?"

"Everywhere," she said.

Justin smiled. "All right. Tonight I'll take you everywhere."

Chapter Fifteen

I want you to come to a party tonight." Laney sat across from Andi's desk, her hand resting on her pregnant belly.

"What party?" Andi asked.

"I'm giving it, and it's a last-minute thing, so I need everyone I can get to come. I have this secret fear, you know, of giving a party and having no one show up, so you'll come, won't you?"

Andi was secretly relieved that she wouldn't have to spend the evening alone. "I'll come, but why are you giving it at the last minute? Is there some special occasion?"

"Yes," she said. "It's an engagement party for Wes's sister Sherry and Clint Jessup. You've met Sherry, haven't you?"

"A couple of times."

"Well, they're crazy in love and have been seeing each other for a pretty long time now, and they just got engaged. She's ecstatic. We all are. And I really wanted to do something special for them, but I'm scared to death the baby will come and put me out of commission for a few weeks. Since the date isn't that far off, and neither is the baby, I thought I'd better go ahead and do it."

"Can I help?" Andi asked.

"No. I couldn't ask you. You're too busy."

"Really," Andi said. "I'd love to." It was the truth, for she couldn't remember the last time she'd had any real female companionship. She had always told herself that she was a goal-setter, and goal-setters didn't have time to spend on friendships. Now, with her father gone and her mother in Europe, she realized that she had been wrong. As both Wes and Justin had pointed out to her, she needed friends. And she needed to be needed.

"Well, okay. If you can be there around five, you can help. I'm inviting about twenty people. It should be fun. Very informal, though."

"I'll be there," Andi said.

Andi was grateful for the distraction that night, and found that the fellowship among Wes and his family and friends was something she had not experienced since college. It had been too long. She didn't know why she had let that part of her life fade into nonexistence.

Sherry was floating with the joy of her new engagement, and brandished her ring to everyone who came in the door. Clint seemed just as happy. As Andi watched them, she found herself wishing with every fiber of her being that she could experience the same joy and permanency.

So why did you treat him so badly the last time you spoke? Why did you let your pride dictate your behavior?

She had been hurt, but that was no reason to turn on him like she had. He had been nothing but kind to her after her father died. He didn't deserve her treatment of him, even if he'd only acted out of a sense of obligation.

Laney sensed her melancholy in the midst of the laughter around them, and asked, "Is everything okay, Andi?"

"Yeah, sure. It's fine."

"Missing Justin?"

She breathed a disbelieving laugh. "Hardly."

"But I thought you two were ..."

"We're not."

There she went again, she thought, kicking herself. Cutting off the connections someone was trying to make with her. Maybe she needed counseling. Maybe she needed prayers. Maybe she needed repentance ... again.

She watched, moved and envious, as Sherry gave Clint the engagement gift she'd gotten him, a fine gold chain that she said symbolized how precious his commitment to her was. He kissed her as she hung it around his neck. Then, in turn, he gave her a charm bracelet that he told her he intended to add to with the name of each of their children as they were born.

Still bubbling with excitement about her wedding plans, Sherry came over to join Andi and Laney. Andi began to relax again. It was easy to feel comfortable with people like these.

"So where's Justin?" Sherry asked Laney. "I figured he'd be here."

"No, he's in New York."

"Oh, well. At least he got to meet Clint the other day. We gave him a ride to that reception. He was late, and—"

"You gave him a ride?" Andi cut in, frowning.

"Yeah. He was a nervous wreck. He'd set out to leave forty-five minutes early and wound up being late."

"Wait a minute," Andi said. "I thought he was with Madeline. She said it was her fault he was late ..."

Laney looked up at Sherry. "You've met Madeline, haven't you? She's the one who painted the cartoons on the wall in the baby's room."

"Oh, yeah! And it *was* her fault. Hers and the other staff members. All four of them left their cars parked behind Justin's and took off to get something to eat. He couldn't get out. He called and asked me to give him a ride. He was literally standing out in front of his house at the curb, in his tux and cummerbund and that cute bow tie, when we drove up. I guess everything worked out, though, huh?"

Andi stared down at the floor for a moment, trying to piece the evening back together. "I was awful to him. I treated him like he'd been late on purpose."

Sherry lowered to the couch next to Laney. "You mean, he didn't tell you why he was late?"

"No," she groaned. "When I pounced on him the minute he walked in, he just clammed up. Justin's not a man who grovels." She closed her eyes and tried to sort it all out.

Across the room, Amy called for her mother, and Laney pulled herself up off of the couch. Andi watched her go to the child and bend over, as much as possible. Amy led her out to the pool to someone who'd been asking about her, and Wes joined them. What a sweet family, she thought. She wondered if she would ever have one of her own.

"You want to see the nursery?" Sherry asked Andi, distracting her.

"Sure," Andi said.

Sherry led her up the stairs and down the hall. "Madeline did a great job. It's all the Khaki's Krewe characters. Justin was too busy to do it, but Madeline did freelance work on the side since Justin didn't pay her very regularly. I guess that's all over now. Glad Laney snagged her for the nursery when she did."

They got to the doorway, and Andi gasped at the beautiful, bold portrayals of the characters she had come to know and love. "This is great. What a lucky baby." She glanced at Sherry. "So you and Laney got to know Madeline pretty well?"

"It's not hard. She's never met a stranger."

"How long has she been with Justin?"

Sherry shrugged. "I'm not sure. A few years, maybe."

Her heart sank. She had hoped that Sherry would set her straight, tell her they weren't an item. "Has she been working for him the same length of time?" she asked, just to clarify.

Sherry shot her a confused look. "That's what I meant. What did you mean? Together, like Clint and me? Wow, I didn't know they were a couple! Madeline never mentioned it."

She felt a little relief at that. She started to dig a little deeper, when she heard someone bolting up the stairs.

Wes ran past them. "Laney's water broke! We have to take her to the hospital!"

Andi caught her breath. "Wes, do you want me to call an ambulance?"

"No, we'll be all right in the car. Sherry, help me get some things packed for her while I call the doctor. Andi, will you stay and close down the party?"

"Sure. Anything else?"

Wes looked a little uncertain for a moment. "No. I'm gonna have another baby!" His eyes filled with tears as he began to laugh. "Is God good, or what?"

Chapter Sixteen

Laney had a boy, and Wes was so thrilled that Andi suspected they heard his shouts of joy all the way to east Texas. As she stood at the nursery window looking in at the little wonder that had caused such commotion, she felt a deep sense of loss. It wasn't that she wasn't happy for Wes and Laney. She was. It was just that the chances of her ever experiencing the excitement of motherhood were looking slimmer and slimmer. She wondered if God had called her to be single, if Promised Land was to be her only offspring. If that was the case, she should be happy, but her faith hadn't been what it should be lately. Joy was difficult in the wake of grief and disappointment.

She leaned her forehead against the glass as a tear rolled down her cheek. *What should I do, Lord? I'm so confused.*

It came to her that she should stop thinking of herself and start concentrating on Justin. He had been kind to her in her time of need, for whatever reason, and now she needed to make amends for the fight they'd had before he left.

The least she could do was offer him some token of regret, some clue that she hadn't meant the ugly things she'd said. Torn between fighting for him and fighting for control over her emotions, she at least wanted to be his friend.

"Hey, those aren't tears, are they?"

She looked up and saw Clint Jessup, Sherry's fiancé. Embarrassed, she wiped her face. "Yeah. He's just so sweet. I got a little emotional."

He smiled and gazed through the window. "He's gonna be a great nephew. I'm gonna be one of those uncles that spoils him rotten. And when Sherry and I have our own . . . man, I'll probably strut around like the king of the world. Wes is so blessed."

She dried her tears and grinned up at him. "Sherry's the lucky one, Clint."

"Yeah?" he asked. "Why do you say that?"

"To be marrying someone who looks so forward to the home and hearth stuff. It's rare, these days."

"Well, look at him," he said, pointing at the baby. "How could you not want that?"

Her smile softened, and she shook her head. "I don't know."

They watched as the nurse took the baby out of his crib.

"You know who'd make a great mom?" Clint asked.

"Who?"

"You. With your organizational skills, you could probably handle a dozen kids. And they'd have such a cool backyard to play in."

Andi laughed. "I think I'll wait until I have a husband."

"That shouldn't be too far off," he said. "I've noticed a glint in the eye of a certain animator . . ."

Her smile faded, but before she could answer, Sherry came running up the hall. "Clint, do you want to come hold the baby?"

Clint dashed toward her. "Are you sure? They're not scared I'll break him?"

Sherry waved for Andi to join them. "Come on, Andi. Laney wants you to hold him too."

Surprised that she would be included in such an intimate family moment, Andi followed them to Laney's room.

Andi gave Justin sufficient time after being back from New York to respond to the gift of apology she'd sent down to him. The little gold statue of Khaki Kangaroo had been custom-made in a frenzy when she'd ordered her jeweler to have it ready immediately.

Hoping the gift had paved her way back into his friendship, she rode the elevator to the sixteenth floor and smiled at the sounds of diligent activity that greeted her. To her left she could hear the tracks being recorded in the sound studio and unable to resist, she followed the high voice of Khaki Kangaroo and peered through the window to see a short, balding man with wild, laughing eyes reading the script. *That's Khaki?* she thought with a laugh. Deciding not to disillusion herself by waiting to see the people behind the other voices, she tore herself away and hurried to Justin's office.

His door was open, but there was no sign of him. Stepping inside, she saw the opened gift box on his desk and wondered where the statue was. Had she missed him on his way up to thank her? Or had he taken it to show his staff?

A woman's gurgling laughter sounded outside and Andi turned around to see Madeline coming out of one of the offices, holding the statue for some of the employees to see. Pivoting in the corridor, she saw Andi. "Did you send us this?" Madeline asked in a lilting voice as she rushed into Justin's office, brandishing the statue like a child with a new Christmas toy. Her thin eyebrows arched in delight and her dark eyes danced.

Andi forced a smile. "I sent it to Justin," she said, tempering her voice with cordiality rather than animosity. "It's kind of a congratulatory gift."

"It's great!" the woman said, straightening her pink headband over her unruly curls. "Wait until he sees it."

"He hasn't seen it?" The anger that she deliberately kept from her voice was apparent in the color rising to her tanned cheeks.

"No," Madeline said nonchalantly. "He's watching one of the Leica reels. You know, checking to make sure the pencil drawings match well with the sound track before they're inked and—"

"I know what a Leica reel is," Andi interrupted.

Madeline set the statue down and shrugged. "Well, I've been taking care of his mail today, trying to help him get caught up on some of the important stuff."

"And that includes opening his gifts?"

"I didn't know it was personal," Madeline said, her voice beginning to edge with "sue me" irritation. "It didn't even have a card."

Andi picked up the statue, turned it upside down, and thrust it toward Madeline. "Wrapped gifts are usually personal. And it doesn't need a card. It's engraved."

Madeline seemed undaunted by the personal touch. Taking it again, with no regard for keeping her fingerprints from smudging it, she read aloud. "'To Justin, for victories without wars. You win, I win . . . Love, Andi.' That's nice," she said mildly, handing the statue back to Andi and leaning against Justin's desk. "Sorry. Guess I goofed. I didn't know." The genuinely apologetic look in her eyes softened Andi's anger a little.

Andi nodded in reluctant acceptance of the apology and set the figure back down. "So," she said, pushing back a wisp of hair that had feathered out of her chignon and seeking a new direction for the conversation. "Did you enjoy New York?"

"It was great," Madeline enthused. "My first time. I went to the School of Visual Arts and found some new animators who are coming next week to start working with us. And then last night we went everywhere." Her shoulders rose dreamily with the last word.

"Celebrating?"

"Yeah," Madeline sighed. "Justin took me out to eat at The Russian Tea Room, and then we went to hear some great music—"

"Where were the others?" Andi cut in, realizing as she spoke that her voice was peppered with jealousy, an emotion she hated worse than any other.

Madeline crossed her arms defensively and narrowed her eyes at the floor. "We couldn't find them. Later we learned that Nathan went to the Brooklyn Tabernacle for a special prayer service they were having. And Gene was with one of the new animators."

Andi swallowed the knot constricting her throat and tried to think rationally. It wasn't a surprise. She had known Justin was taking Madeline with him and she had known why. But coming to terms with their involvement was going to take time. It was hard to fight when her opponent didn't consider her a threat, she thought miserably. Either Madeline was naive or didn't care that Andi and Justin had spent so much time together before New York. But Andi couldn't accept it so easily. Though there had been no declarations of love, no kiss, not even many touches except when she'd been distraught. Justin had done nothing that a brother wouldn't have done. She was the stupid one for reading so much into it.

Before she could give it more thought, she heard Justin coming through the outside offices, answering questions on his way in and giving mild commands to the employees who scurried efficiently around him. An aura of self-confidence and success radiated from him, though the light blue shirt and tan slacks he wore gave a casual effect to his unself-conscious style. His eyes sparkled with reeling thoughts, but when he stepped into the office and saw Andi, the shutters closed visibly over them, and his cool hello left her feeling shunned and alone.

"Hi," she said. When Madeline didn't make a move to leave, Andi glanced uncomfortably at her, then dragged her eyes back to Justin. "I came to congratulate you."

"Thanks," he said, a cool smile lighting his eyes a degree.

Clearing her throat, Madeline grinned awkwardly and backed out of the office. "I have work to do. I'll see you folks later."

The obvious way she left the two of them alone bewildered Andi, and she watched her leave in amazement. Was she so secure with Justin that she trusted him completely? The idea was disheartening, for it had been her experience that self-confidence was the best defense against adversity. And if that was the case here, Andi was distressingly unarmed. It might be easier to deal with, Andi thought with chagrin, if she could make herself dislike the woman. But despite her efforts, she couldn't manage to do even that. "How was your trip?" she asked finally.

"Great," Justin said, setting down the papers he held and shuffling them absently on his desk. "Gave me plenty of time to think."

From the deliberate way he tried to ignore her, Andi had no doubts that she had been the subject of those thoughts. "Me too," she said in a hoarse voice, then cleared her throat. "I've realized I was a little . . . short with you before you left, and I shouldn't have been."

"It's okay," Justin said, bringing his vacant eyes up to hers. "I won't let it affect our business relationship."

The tone of his voice ranked somewhere between sarcasm and sincerity, and not prepared for such a comment, Andi couldn't answer. There seemed nothing more to say as they held each other's gaze across the room. Finally Justin looked down at his desk again.

"What's this?" he asked, noticing the small, polished statue on his desk. He picked it up and examined the smooth golden lines of his star character.

"A gift," Andi said carefully, waiting for some sign of pleasure in his eyes, but there was none. "I'm afraid Madeline got to it first."

At the mention of the dark-haired beauty, Justin broke out in a grin. "Never leave a wrapped gift around Madeline. She can't stand the suspense, and she'll find some excuse to open it every time. She's the same way with secrets, I'm afraid. But she means well." As he spoke, he unbuttoned his cuffs and began rolling his sleeves up corded forearms, shifting the statue from one hand to the other. "What is it? Solid gold?"

Andi nodded proudly. It had cost a fortune, but it would be worth it if he would just flash her that smile that would tell her he forgave her for her outburst before his trip.

A muscle rippled in his jaw. "I'll pay you back for it," he said, setting it down. "We can afford to decorate our own offices now."

A suffocating lump formed in Andi's throat and her smile faded. "I don't want you to pay me back, Justin. It was a gift."

"I don't want your gifts," he parried, lowering himself into his chair. Then, as if catching his bitterness, he set the kangaroo down and raked a hand through his dark hair.

"It was for your staff," she lied quickly, desperate to keep all painful inflections from her voice. "From my staff. I'll be sure and tell them you appreciate it."

The words seemed to change things, yet he studied her with suspicion. "Oh. I thought . . . Well, in that case I accept.

For my staff. I'll be certain to thank your people for it myself."

"Don't bother," Andi said, lowering to one of his chairs and crossing her arms, as if somehow that would protect her from any more blows. "It was really no big deal."

Justin picked up the statue again, seeming to fondle it with deeper appreciation now that he knew it was impersonal. As he turned it over in his hands, Andi prayed that he wouldn't see the inscription. Maybe he would never see it. Silently, she lashed herself for making the foolish move, wishing that just this once she had not been so impetuous. "If you have time, I'd like to touch base with you about a few things," she said, hoping to distract him.

He set the kangaroo down and leaned back in his seat, bringing his frosted eyes back to hers. "All right," he said.

Andi propped her elbows on her knees, desperately trying to relax. "I kept B.J. pretty busy while you were gone. We got a good bit of work done on the designs for the automated figures, and I talked to him about some possible changes in your settings if you got the network contract. He seemed to like my ideas."

Justin bit the inside of his cheek and drummed his fingers on his desk. "I haven't had time to talk to him much since I've been here today. I've been in meetings all morning. You mind filling me in?"

Andi nodded. "I'd like for you to move your characters from the farm setting where you have them to a sort of Promised Land-type setting for both the feature film and the television segments. Your segments could have to do with areas of the park. The Noah's Ark area, or Jonah's Ride, or Jacob's Ladder, or Canaan."

Justin leaned back and laid his palms down on his desk. "Andi, I've been considering ways to bring Promised Land into my cartoons. But *I* am the animator. I'm the one who comes up with the ideas. Not you."

"Fine," Andi clipped. "Then talk to me about them. We're in this together, Justin."

Justin tapped the tips of his fingers together, a frown buckling his brows. "I kind of liked the idea of reworking some of your rides so that they fit more into my farm theme. I can't exactly see Ned the nearsighted farmer trekking up Mt. Sinai."

Her feigned composure shattered like crystal. "You want to rework my rides? Do you know what you're asking?"

"Not to any great extent," he said, stemming further objections with his hands. "We wouldn't reverse any of the progress already made on them. But since most of them aren't finished yet, there's plenty of room for improvement on the original plans."

"Improvement? I have some of the best creative minds in the world helping plan my park. It would be easier to change the cartoons."

"Forget it," Justin snapped. "If it doesn't fit my story line, I won't even consider it."

"That isn't what B.J. said," Andi flung back. "He and the others have already come up with ideas for the stories."

Justin dropped his hands with a loud thud. "Who gave you the right to give assignments to my staff? I don't like being undermined. I'm the animation director here, not B.J. They're my characters, and *I* make the decisions."

Andi's voice flared louder than she expected. "You gave me the right when you told me that B.J. could make decisions for you while you were gone."

Justin sprang out of his chair and slammed it back against his desk. "I didn't know you'd go behind my back and try to rewrite the scripts for me. There's timing to consider, and the possibilities for gags, and the potential for a different story each week without overdoing the same old things. You think just because you dreamed up Promised Land that you can come in here and do the same thing with my cartoons? Forget it! I'd rather let you sue me!"

Andi stood up and cast a murderous stare at the man across the desk. "I might just have to do that if you don't stop attacking me every time I approach you with an idea! There are decisions that have to be made immediately. Like how to handle the advertising for the park. Are your characters going to be associated with that or not? And the cartoon that coincides with our opening. Since I'm paying for that, I expect to be in on the planning stages. That's how I work, Justin! Like it or not. And we can make it as easy or as difficult as we want to. But as long as we keep butting heads, neither of us will make any headway, and we'll have to give up on this merger as a bad idea."

Justin sucked in a dramatic breath. "Do you think there's really hope of that?"

For lack of anything else to lash out at, Andi knocked her chair over with a crash and pointed a shaking finger at him. "There's always hope," she seethed. "But if I were you I'd think about it for a while! And when you think you're ready to sit down and discuss this reasonably without blowing a fuse every time you disagree with me, then you know where to find me!"

The door slammed behind her, leaving Justin fuming with impotent rage. After a moment, he stepped out into the open area of his offices and thundered out Madeline's name, ordering her to gather his senior animators for a conference. "I'll come up with some ideas all right," he mumbled, jerking the chair off the floor and setting it upright with a clatter. "But I won't need Andi Sherman to help me do it."

Chapter Seventeen

It was past midnight when the exhausted animators convinced Justin to sleep on the ideas they'd formulated. Gene was stretched catatonically across the table that was cluttered and stacked with discarded drawings, and B.J. sat humped over the drafting table in the corner of Justin's office. Madeline, the only one still awake, had gone to check on some of the things the engineers needed to know about the robot designs before morning. Nathan was half asleep sitting on the floor, his head leaned back against the wall, a mountain of crumpled paper covering the carpet around him. But Justin still paced in front of his desk, studying the drawings laid out across it, searching them for flaws.

Perfect, he thought, adrenaline rushing through his blood, making it even more unbelievable to him that the others could have dropped out on him like this. They'd found a way to incorporate all the different themes of Andi's park into his stories, and the kickoff cartoon on ABC that would coincide with the park's opening would be an international invitation to Promised Land. He'd discovered a way to have the characters still live on their eventful farm, but instead of making Ned simply a nearsighted farmer bumbling around his own farm, they would send him through time warps in which he experienced real biblical stories in his klutzy, slapstick way, getting him into trouble from which his farm animals had to rescue him. Khaki Kangaroo would be his sidekick, stirring up more trouble and getting them into the thick of all of the greatest events of the Bible. Their travels could take them to other countries, leading to adventures related to Promised Land's "Hands Across the Sea" area; or other planets, relating to the "He Also Made the Stars" portion; or to oceans, associating the cartoons with the Jonah and Nineveh sections of the park. The adventures were limitless, and the basic gags and story lines would require very little alteration, since the villainous troll would be swept into the travels with them in each episode, representing the ever-present Satan tugging them toward his own ways. The potential for evangelism was limitless, and he could even see parents watching the cartoons with their children and learning growth principles about their own walk with Christ. Principles he would do well to learn himself, he mused.

Biting his victorious smile, Justin began to stack the drawings. "You guys go on home," he said absently as he slid them into an envelope. "I'm going to put these on Andi's secretary's desk. She'll hit her with them first thing tomorrow." Caught in his thoughts and exuberance, he didn't realize as he hurried across the floor that not one of the animators had stirred.

Andi sat with her bare feet curled under her on her office sofa, studying her father's Bible that lay open in her lap. She had done it again. She had let her pride drive her, had forgotten all the regrets and apologies ... Once again, she had allowed them to become enemies.

She'd knocked off work hours ago, since she didn't have the heart for it, and had decided to spend some time in prayer. She had wept and confessed it all to God—all the jealousy and pride, all the lies and games she had played with Justin, all the bad feelings and bitterness, all the sorrow and hopelessness.

And she had confessed that she still hadn't gotten into step with Christ, even though she had seen that it was the problem. She had put her work before him, and she had let her obsessions with Justin distract her.

So now she had gone back to the Bible, the only source from which she could get real strength, the only place she could go for real advice. As she read, a peace came over her. God had forgiven her. It wasn't too late to get things right.

She could have taken the Bible home to read, but she had decided to do it here.

She wasn't tired, and lately she'd avoided her apartment until she was too exhausted to think. Life had been disturbingly empty since her father's death and Justin's trip to New York. There had been no direction for her, no place to go after hours. She missed her father desperately, as well as the bland hospital food and her quiet friendships with the nurses and doctors who had attended him. She missed the few days she had spent with Justin, the supportive smiles, the gentle touches. And she knew she would never know those things again.

A shadow in the area outside her office startled her, and she sat up, alarmed, as the dark shape of a man came into view.

"We're suffering from the same disease," Justin mumbled in a gravelly voice, making her exhale in relief as he stepped into her yellow circle of light. In a weary stance, he leaned his wrist against the doorjamb over his head and set the hand with the envelope on his hip, but his eyes were bright and wide-awake.

"What disease is that?" she asked, trying to stop the smile creeping across her face as she sensed gratefully that he had put the morning's fight behind him.

"Workaholism." Stepping inside, he plopped down on the opposite end of the sofa and threw his arm across the back. "I didn't think it was possible that anyone else could be working this late, and here you are."

Andi sighed and set her Bible on the cushions between them. "I just can't seem to turn off my mind and go home. Is it that way for you?"

"You know it is," he whispered, raking his hand through his hair, his blue eyes beginning to smile in answer. His eyes swept over her, and her hand gravitated self-consciously to her hair. It was still up, but stray wisps had eased out of their pins and feathered around her neck and face in slight disarray.

Their eyes locked for a long, quiet moment, and finally Justin tore his eyes from her and looked down at the envelope he'd brought. "I've been working on this," he said in his lazy baritone. "I think we've come up with something you'll like, but it can wait until morning if you're too tired. I was just coming to leave it on your secretary's desk."

As if she'd just been tempted with a gift, her smile grew with anticipation, and she leaned forward to get it.

Forcing his attention to the drawings, he explained in a soft voice what each one represented, and the new twist in the story line, and the way the park would be an important part of the cartoons. Andi's eyes glittered with appreciation as she turned the pages, and she laughed under her breath at each situation. When she had finally seen them all, she handed them back to Justin. "Brilliant," she said. "It's everything I wanted."

"Even though you didn't think of it?" he asked, cocking a heavy brow.

"Justin, when are you going to learn?" she asked, her eyes luminous with conviction. "I'm not out to be your enemy.

It's just that I don't like settling for things. Everything can always be improved on."

"But you don't have to be the one who improves everything, Andi," he said without rancor. "The world won't deflate if Andi Sherman rests. And it won't fall to pieces if you miss something. You've held it all together beautifully, but you've got to trust me to know what's best about my part in all this."

Andi leaned her head back against the cushions and looked off at nothing across the room, a sigh punctuating her thoughts. "I know. It's just that it all means so much to me. It's so important."

"I know." His voice was soft with gentle understanding. "It means a lot to me too."

When quiet settled between them, tension mounting to the point that there was no place for the conversation to move except into the realm of the personal, Justin decided it was time to go.

Standing up, he took the drawings and gave a careless, feline stretch of his arms, starting toward the door. "Guess I'd better go get some sleep so I'll be worth something tomorrow," he said.

Was it disappointment he saw flash in the emerald depths of her eyes or only fatigue, he wondered for an instant?

"Me too," she said, picking her Bible back up. "Thanks for coming by." Her voice was so soft, so cautious, that he wasn't sure how to read it. Pushing the ambiguity in her tone and her expression out of his mind, he strode back through the darkness to the elevator and rode down to his floor.

B.J. and Nathan had gone home, but Gene still lay like a cadaver across the table in Justin's office. He shouldn't have worked them so hard today, he thought with a smile as he sat down behind his desk. Only people like himself and Andi, who did it because they couldn't help themselves, should be forced to stay this late. He considered waking Gene, then decided against it. He seemed to be sleeping soundly, and waking him to go home and sleep seemed to defeat the purpose.

His mind drifted four floors above him to Andi curled up on that sofa all alone. He had wanted so much to linger there with her. But she had made it clear before his trip that she didn't want a relationship with him. Still ... there was something in her eyes when she looked at him ...

His eyes fell to the golden form of Khaki Kangaroo. He picked it up and turned it over in his hands as he thought what a jerk he had been when he saw it this morning. Instead of realizing that it had taken a caring person to dream up a gift like that, much less execute it, he had discounted it as cheap strategy aimed at ... what? Appeasing him long enough to spring her ideas on him? Her ideas hadn't been so far off base. Even if it had come from her staff, he knew it had been Andi's idea. And that meant something.

As he turned it carefully in his hand, the light of his lamps played softly off the bottom of the kangaroo. He squinted and held the statue closer to the bulb, trying to make out the letters inscribed in script. "To Justin, for victories without wars. You win, I win ... Love Andi."

You win, I win, he chanted mentally. From the song by Jackson Browne, Andi's longtime favorite singer. *You win, I win ... we lose.* Was that what she had meant? Or was it just a rebuttal of the thought she'd uttered days ago? *Neither of us can win when we're together*.

Whatever the message meant, it sent his heart careening. It *was* a personal gift, and he had been so ungrateful that he'd humiliated her into lying about it, only proving the point of her engraved message. *You win, I win ...* We lose. Again the words flitted through his mind. Was that why she had cut things off with him? Had his constant resistance to her ideas—his determination to always be right—convinced her that was the only way?

He looked at the door and wondered if he should follow his impulse to go back to her office. What would he say?

Deciding that he'd know what to say when he got there, he dashed into the elevator hoping he wasn't too late to catch her.

She was just where he had left her, but as he approached her door, he saw her simply staring with sad, sullen eyes across the room to the large window. The lonely glare in her green eyes disappeared at his knock, and she flashed a welcoming smile so convincing that he wondered if he'd imagined the sorrow.

Walking in, he answered her smile. "I was thinking," he said softly. "What do you say we find a pizza place that delivers this late? We owe ourselves a celebration for the amazing thing that happened tonight, and frankly, I forgot to eat."

Andi laughed with bewilderment, the sound playing like wind chimes in his heart. "What amazing thing?" she asked. "Wasn't it an ordinary night?"

"Not by any stretch of these vivid imaginations of ours," he said, "because tonight we finally agreed on something."

Chapter Eighteen

We did agree, didn't we?" Andi exulted, crossing her feet Indian-style on the sofa and facing Justin as she munched on the pizza that had been delivered moments earlier. It was amazing how hungry she suddenly was, when earlier she'd had no appetite at all. "And without casualties."

"Yes, we did." The lines at the corners of his eyes webbed with his grin.

"Should I send out a press release?" she teased.

He chuckled. "Somehow I don't think the press could appreciate the significance."

"Well," she said, leaning her head back against the tall sofa arm. "We'd just have to make it interesting enough." Sighing, she studied the ceiling, as if reading the headlines there. "'Sherman and Pierce Reach Detente.'"

Justin laughed. "A little too strong, I think. How about 'Pierce Admits to Being Jerk?'"

She looked at him with a question on her face. "Why would you say that?"

He looked down at the rough lines on his palms. "I saw the inscription on the statue," he said. "It was sweet, and there's no other word for me but 'jerk.'"

Andi almost choked on her pizza. "I've called you that under my breath a few times. But I'm sure that's no worse than what you would say about me."

"Well, let's see." Justin glanced at the same spot on the ceiling where she'd just found her headlines. "Twenty-nine-year-old creative genius who knows what she wants and has the uncanny ability to make others want it, too." Her pleased smile urged him on, and he brought his sparkling eyes back to her. "Her strength is staggering, her will is unwavering, her drive is . . ."

"Dreadful," Andi provided.

Justin gave her that one and continued, the ticklish edge of laughter lacing his voice. "She's unpredictable, unforgettable, indecipherable . . ." Her wide-eyed, surprised expression stopped his heart, making his smile dissolve over a long sigh as his eyes riveted deeply into hers, " . . . and she has eyes that could either freeze or melt your heart, depending on her mood."

Andi tried to still the pounding in her chest and countered the compliment with drollery. "Do you think they'd print that?"

"Well," he said with a lazy shrug. "Maybe if it came as a direct quote."

"No." She studied the pattern of pepperonis on her pizza. "I doubt you could ever make yourself say that in public. And without sheer exhaustion, I'm certain I wouldn't be hearing it now." She grinned and stretched her feet out on the couch until her arches almost touched Justin's thighs. "Besides," she said, quirking her brows, "the press has forgotten all about me. It's that new animator on the premises that has them all talking."

"And have you been talking back?" he probed with a grin that seemed to bring sunlight into the shadowed room.

"Of course," she teased. "You know me. Always happy to cooperate with the media."

"What sort of things did they want to know?" he asked, knowing he shouldn't.

"The usual," she said with a mischievous curve of her lips. "Your phone number, your clothing size, whether you sleep in pajamas . . ."

Justin's eyes danced with laughter. "As if you'd know. And what did you tell them?"

"I told them that you rarely sleep at all." She brought her soda to her lips to hide her devilish grin. "But that when you do, it's usually fully clothed and sitting up straight."

"Well, at least I dress comfortably. T-shirts and jeans aren't so tough to sleep in, sitting up straight or not." He looked down at the dress shirt he'd worn today because of all his meetings. "I thought I did pretty good today, keeping my shirttail tucked in for most of the day."

"The fact that you're wearing shirts that *have* tails now is a major accomplishment."

He grinned. "It is, isn't it?"

Their eyes locked across the distance of the couch as their laughter ebbed into smiling sighs.

When the quiet became too tense, too awkward, Andi pulled herself off of the couch and went back to the pizza box. "So we're friends again?" she asked, turning back to Justin.

"For a while," he conceded, watching her with unyielding regard as she refilled both glasses with the canned Cokes they'd gotten from the machine downstairs.

Trying to steady her hand under his careful scrutiny, Andi set the can back down and took her place on the sofa again. "Incredible," she said with open honesty. "I'd almost forgotten what it was like to be either in a state of war or a temporary cease-fire all the time. Until the accident, Daddy kept me going, but it's been relatively boring around here since."

Justin feigned a hurt look. "You mean I'm not the only one who's ever gotten your temper to the boiling point?"

Andi smiled. "You know better than that. Dad was almost as insufferable as you sometimes." Another moment of quiet settled between them as they drank, watching each other over their glasses. "I've been curious," Andi said finally. "I went eight years without hearing your name, and then all of a sudden you were here. Where have you been? What have you been doing?"

Justin shrugged and studied the fizz in his soda. "I've been planning my strategy all this time. Perfecting my craft, I guess, and deciding exactly how I was going to spring my talent on the world." He took a drink and offered an indolent grin as if remembering foolish days. "Trouble was, not everybody saw what I had as talent. And I sometimes wondered if it wasn't more of a curse than a gift, because no matter how bad things got, they never got bad enough to quit."

Andi nodded, clearly understanding that kind of stubbornness. "Even when your best characters were stolen?"

Surprise skittered across his eyes, instantly making her regret her question. "You knew about that?"

She shrugged and gave an apologetic nod. "I found out when we were trying to buy your characters. It proved to me that I'd have to give more than I wanted, because I knew you'd never risk that again."

Justin breathed a laugh. "You were right. Those were bad times."

"But you came through it."

Justin leaned his head back, letting the past flit through his mind as if it were the first time he'd considered it objectively. "It was revenge, I think," he admitted. "When the jerk hired my animators out from under me to continue my series, all I wanted to do was get even, make them all eat their hearts out. Funny thing was, when the series failed, I was crushed and satisfied at the same time. I hated to see my creation bite the dust, but I was glad that God had taken care of things for me. The whole thing gave me new motivation."

Narrowing her eyes, Andi sought bitterness in his expression, but there was none. "Motivation to get even?"

Justin contemplated the question with a twinkle of surprise in his eyes. "You know, it hasn't even crossed my mind since I've been here. I guess I have other motivation now."

Andi laid her head against the cushion and smiled at his frank self-appraisal. He was happy, she thought, and that lent her a fragile bit of joy.

"Madeline's partially responsible for my getting back on my feet," he said, sending her spirits crashing to earth as his eyes softened with the thought of his assistant. "She's been with me for five years. She's the only animator who didn't abandon me, even though they offered her more than I could pay her. She had to take a lot of freelance work to supplement her income while she kept working for me, but she never complained. I'll never forget that." His eyes were soft as he spoke of her, and Andi would have sacrificed everything she owned to have him speak as tenderly of her.

Closing her eyes against the pain of too much honesty, Andi leaned her head back and clutched her glass until her knuckles whitened. No wonder he cared for Madeline. She offered no threat, no demands.

Relaxing, he went on with his quiet rambling. "When I get a big enough staff and enough money, I'm going to start work on the feature film Madeline and I have been planning for years. It's my biggest dream. It'll take a few years to get it to the stage I want it since it'll be fully animated, but it'll be worth it." His voice warmed through the chill in her heart, and his new belief in dreams he'd shunned when she'd known him before gave her a glimmer of hope, though it had little to do with her.

"That shouldn't be too far off, should it?"

A wry laugh contradicted her. "The budget for a high-quality film like that's in the millions. I couldn't even borrow that much right now."

"How about investors?" she asked.

Justin found that amusing. "Who? I'm the new kid on the block. No one really knows who I am yet."

"I would invest," Andi said. "I know the depth of your imagination, and I believe you could do whatever you wanted." Even if Madeline was part of it, she thought miserably. Sitting up straight, she leaned toward him with more conviction. "I mean it, Justin. I'd like to invest."

The gradual hardening of his features told her she'd made a grave error in judgment. "Our agreement excluded the feature film," he said as though offended. "If you invest in it, that will change things. I had that clause put into our agreement for a reason. I don't want you having a stake in everything I do. I can do it without you."

Andi sank back onto the couch and brought a hand to her forehead to hide the mist of self-deprecation filling her eyes. "Of course you can," she whispered. Forcing a smile, she breathed a laugh. "You'd think I'd know better by now." Her smile faded into regret, and she asked, "Why is it so hard for us to get along, Justin?" She knew the honest question would require an honest answer.

"Sometimes we've gotten along real well," he said, as if he'd given the matter a great deal of thought. "But I guess those times are few and far between. Mostly because we're both stubborn and creative people. And because of our past."

"But we've both changed," she breathed out earnestly. Pulling her feet up, she bent her knees and folded her elbows across them. "Everything's on a larger scale here." Her eyes sparkled as she glanced out the window at the darkness that she saw as an empty slate, waiting to be filled in. "We're making history with dreams. God's using us both. We're working toward the same goal, even if we have different ways of going about reaching it."

Justin rubbed his eyes ruefully. "It's easy to lose focus of that goal," he said. "Other things can get in the way ..."

"What other things?"

Before he could answer, a blaring, screeching alarm cut off her words, startling them both. Andi bolted off of the couch and flew to the computer on her desk. "Oh, no! It's a fire," she muttered, urgently punching buttons to discover the source.

Justin fled to the window, where he could see the hazy light of flames and the small Promised Land fire engines' lights at the scene. "Looks like the Hands Across the Sea area," he said, but Andi was already out the door, shoes in hand.

"Come on! We've got to get over there!"

Justin followed her onto the elevator and punched the first-floor button. The ride down was agonizingly slow, giving an open view of dark floors. "If the fire has reached the robots, we're in trouble," she said when they reached the first floor and rushed out across the lobby floor.

The moment they reached the humid night air, Andi knew that whatever hope she'd had was futile. The vicinity was lit in a yellow haze as flames danced from the roof of the structure. Without looking for an electric car, she took off on foot, running as if her park depended on her speed.

Behind her, she heard the wailing sirens of the fire department, and thanked God that her security guards had called them in time to keep the other buildings from going up. The trucks whisked past her and screeched to a halt in front of the building, and a dozen firemen dispersed and began to work efficiently to help the Promised Land fire fighters stifle the blaze.

Chapter Nineteen

When she reached the burning building, Andi grabbed one of her security guards. "What happened?"

"I don't know," the man shouted over the noise. "I can't even figure out who set off the alarm."

Justin couldn't hear the exchange of words, but when Andi darted off through the men, stopping at each security guard and shooting questions that most answered with a shake of the head or a helpless shrug, he went after her.

Scurrying activity and stretched hoses slowed his progress, and an instant of panic welled within him as he saw Andi move dangerously close to the entrance, peering anxiously inside as if she could stop the flames with sheer will.

"Keep her out of there!" one of the firemen shouted, his hands clamped on a nozzle as Justin pushed past him. "It may not look bad in there, but that roof is about to go any minute!"

Andi moved closer to the building. Still trying to reach her, Justin screamed, "Andi!" But his voice didn't penetrate the dazed, horrified look on her face. Violent in his efforts to reach her, Justin pushed people out of his way, watching, dismayed, as she shouted something he couldn't hear, then tore insanely into the building, the gray haze of smoke swallowing her. "ANDI!" His grated voice pierced the night, but it was too late for her to hear.

The men around him seemed to freeze, the flames seemed to stop in their heavenward reaches, the smoke seemed to become a drawn curtain between Andi and him. Fear stampeded through him, and he had but one panic-stricken thought. Andi was going to die in those flames. He shot through the men and into the building, tearing off his shirt as he ran.

The only sounds inside were those of crackling, popping flames overhead and along the walls. The wide open space of the center—waiting to be filled with water before the park's opening—was without flames, but the smoke was quickly reaching suffocating proportions. The automated figures built on the sides of the room were melting masses of machinery slowly shrinking in flames that pranced regally around them. Were they what Andi had run in here for?

"Andi!" The word choked him, and he coughed the smoke out of his lungs as he went deeper into the building, pressing his shirt against his nose to filter the polluted air.

A muffled sound drew his eyes toward the back of the building where the flames were already the victors. Against the blinding red glow, he saw Andi's silhouette, staggering as she struggled to drag something behind her.

"Let it go!" he blared as he careened toward her.

She didn't have to answer, for when he reached her, he saw that she was dragging Madeline, limp and unconscious, behind her.

Squatting down, Justin pulled the woman's limp weight onto his shoulders and caught Andi, wavering with dizziness before she doubled over in a fit of coughing. "Hold this against your face," he ordered, thrusting his shirt into her hands. "Now stay low and get out of here!"

Keeping an eye on the unsteady ceiling, he ran behind her. Boards smashed and walls crumbled behind them as they ran through the hell-like chamber, the furnace heat of the blaze pursuing them, until finally they ran into the spraying water and were grabbed by the firemen who had come in after them.

Madeline was loaded into an ambulance that had pulled up while they were inside, and she began to come to as they began to administer oxygen. There were no apparent burns on her body. It was the smoke that had almost killed her.

Andi and Justin, strangled and coughing at the sudden rush of oxygen in polluted lungs, were immediately treated by the paramedics.

Andi's face was dark with black smoke and water, and her wet hair fell from its pins to tumble wildly around her shoulders. When they could both breathe without the oxygen masks, Justin took her by the arms, shaking her gently as his mist-filled eyes raked over her with furious relief. "You stupid thing," he raged softly through his teeth, emotion racking his voice. "How could you do that?"

"I'm sorry, Justin," she said, her voice raw and hoarse. "I saw her moving near the back of the building, just before she collapsed, and there wasn't any time to waste."

"You both could have been killed," he moaned, crushing her against him, his arms trembling with the aftermath of fear.

She leaned into his bare wet chest, closing her arms around his waist, only beginning to feel the terror seep into her now that she knew they were safe. "So could you."

He rocked back and forth, holding her as if his arms could keep her from being swallowed into the flames again. "What if I had lost you? What if—?"

"I'm okay," she whispered, tears burning down her cheeks. His heart was slamming against her, and she looked up at him to see painful tears making paths through the soot on his face.

"Don't ever do that again," he whispered, still rocking her back and forth. His swallow came with great effort when she moved her hands up to frame his face. Tears still welled in the blue depths of his eyes, and his breathing was deep and labored. Without thinking, she pressed a kiss to his dry lips, and his arms closed tighter around her. "Andi, I love you," he murmured against her ear.

Although one of the most important buildings in her park was crashing and consuming into glowing embers, with flames threatening to conquer the beloved buildings nearby, and the men were yelling and the machinery screaming and sirens blaring, Andi felt strangely at peace.

Justin's voice was all she heard.

Chapter Twenty

Andi washed the lather from her hair, closing her eyes and letting warm jets of water beat down on her face. Had the evening been a bad nightmare or a poignant dream? Had Hands Across the Sea really burned down while she stood helplessly watching? Had Justin really said he loved her?

No dream, she thought with a confusing twang of pain throbbing in her heart. Those things had happened. But she mustn't take them out of perspective. Justin had just seen her run into a den of flames, and as her friend, he had been frightened. Of course he loved her. Friends always did. And they had restated that friendship in her office tonight. His fear and relief had made him say things that he might regret later, unless she took the words the way they were meant.

But the fact that he'd clung to her, not Madeline, had been confusing. He had been worried about his assistant, had even insisted on rushing to the hospital behind the ambulance to make sure she was all right. But it had been Andi's hand he held as they stood over Madeline's bed, and he'd made no attempt to hide his affection for Andi from Madeline.

"You saved my life," Madeline had told her in a raspy voice. "I can't believe you saw me. I was so stupid. I was in one of the other buildings critiquing the robot designs so the engineers could have my report first thing tomorrow, when I smelled smoke. When I realized it was in Hands Across the Sea, I set off the alarm and was trying to save the robots. But I couldn't get them out, and the smoke was so thick. If you hadn't come, I'd be dead, Andi. You're a real hero."

She reached out to take Andi's hand, and Andi squeezed hers. "I couldn't have done it without Justin."

"Yeah, I know. But you're the one who rushed in. I don't know how to repay you. Is eternal friendship enough, you think?"

Andi smiled. "Sure, it is."

Later, as she stepped out of the shower, she asked herself how she could have ever disliked a woman like that. And she was confused now ... confused about what Madeline meant to Justin ... whether he had ever been involved with her or not ... whether she was Andi's biggest threat or greatest ally. She just didn't know anymore.

After she was dressed, Andi towel-dried her hair and ran a comb through it, postponing the moment of facing Justin now that things were calm. He was out there in her living room, waiting for her. He seemed to want to comfort her, to help her through her second catastrophe in a matter of days. She hated being so needy, yet she couldn't deny that she loved having Justin fill those needs.

Going into her living room, she saw that Justin was on her couch. "Come here," he said. She went and sat down next to him, and he gazed at her, tracing a finger down her hairline and over her ear, pushing back the long, damp strands. "Feel better?"

"I guess," she whispered. "Until tomorrow, when I have to face the damage in broad daylight, and answer all the questions, and make plans to start all over ..." Tears sprang to her eyes, and she closed them and touched her forehead with trembling fingertips. "Oh, Justin, I don't want to be your enemy tomorrow. I want to be your friend, even when there's no catastrophe hanging over us."

"We aren't really enemies," Justin said quietly. "Rivals, maybe, but not enemies."

Closing her eyes, Andi lay her head on the back of the sofa. "What on earth would we be rivaling for?"

Justin's eyes seemed to grow distant as he thought that over. Finally, he looked at her with a look of deep sadness in his eyes. "Our hearts," he said quietly.

Andi opened her eyes and pulled herself partially up, a soft frown transforming her face. "Justin, I've never tried to take your heart from you."

"You never had to try."

The words stopped her heart and paralyzed her limbs. His eyes were eloquent with blatant emotion and painful honesty, and she had to force herself to remember she wasn't the only woman in his life.

"It's ironic," he added, in that soft, hypnotic voice. "You're the one human being in my life that I can truly say has given me the greatest joy and the deepest sadness. And so many of the lessons God has taught me in my life have been somehow taught through my relationship with you."

Her heart threatened to explode. "I'm sorry for the sadness, Justin."

"Yeah, me, too," he whispered.

"My mother told me I needed to ask for your forgiveness," she said, desperately trying to hold back the tears, "and I think she's right. I never apologized for believing you had taken money to break up with me. But you can't know how much I've regretted it. I'm so sorry."

He nodded. "What hurt the most is that you thought I could be capable of that."

"I wasn't thinking clearly. I was angry and hurt that you'd left, and my father offered a quick explanation that made sense. I didn't think it through."

"I know," he said. "And you trusted your father. That's how it's supposed to be."

"Fathers aren't supposed to lie."

"No, they aren't."

"But he changed, Justin. And if he had been able to, he would have asked for your forgiveness. Just like I'm doing."

Justin's smile was fragile with emotion. "You've got it, Andi. And he's got it, too."

A tear spilled over her lashes, and she reached up to wipe it away.

Justin took her hand away from her face, laced his fingers through hers, and gazed down into her wet eyes that held such deep longing.

Slowly, he lowered his face to hers. As their lips touched, the past became present, with eight long, haunting years of collected dreams to heighten it. The power they had used against each other melded into the power of that one kiss, as they each left indelible prints on the other's heart.

She broke the kiss and dropped her forehead against his neck.

"What's wrong?" he asked.

"This," she whispered. "It's the way we come together. I don't want you to care for me only when I've been through an ordeal."

"You know it's more than that," Justin said, pushing a frustrated hand through his hair. "It's just that I fight it, and it's just when you need me that I can't seem to fight anymore. It's only then that it doesn't scare me so much."

Still, her doubts lingered. Hot tears welled in her eyes, and she whispered in a broken voice, "I have to ask you about Madeline."

His head came up, those expressive eyes harboring no sign of deceit. "What do you mean?"

"Who is she to you, Justin?" She lowered her face to spare herself the pain of seeing the truth.

But when his hands framed her face and drew it back to his, she saw only a gentle, bewildered expression. "She's one of my closest friends," he whispered. "Has been for years. But that's all."

"But ... I overheard a conversation. I shouldn't have. I should have just turned the other way, but it happened. I heard her telling you that she didn't want you ruining what you had built together for the sake of some overblown sense of obligation to me."

Justin's fingers closed her mouth, his eyes becoming luminous with conviction. "Andi, she was talking about our work. I had told her that I wanted to put off the trip to New York, that I wasn't ready to leave you yet. Plus I'd had a change of heart about sticking around and working with you on the robotics. I was thinking of sending someone else in my place. Madeline was afraid I was risking the ABC deal if I didn't go, and she said I had a false sense of obligation. She wasn't talking about our relationship, Andi. She was talking about business. And the truth is, I *was* using business as an excuse not to leave you."

"Then you and Madeline are not an item?"

He laughed aloud. "No! We never have been. She's like a sister in a lot of ways. I could never think of Madeline that way."

A soft "oh" whispered through her lips, and Justin studied the relief in her face as understanding crept into his eyes.

"That was why you denied what had been happening between us," he said in an amazed voice, as if the pieces were finally coming together. "It was wounded pride, and I thought it was business."

"I'm sorry," she whispered, "I'm so sorry."

"But do you believe me?" he whispered.

"I believe you." The words came on a breath of gratitude.

They stared at each other for a long moment, and finally Justin said, "You have to know something, Andi. I love you. I think I always have."

Uninhibited joy burst inside her. "I have too, Justin," she whispered. "I've never stopped."

He reached up to touch a fallen strand of hair, twirled it around a finger, used it to pull her face closer to his. His lips touched hers again, then retreated. His eyes were full of turmoil, full of surrender, and she yearned to trust what she read there.

His voice quivered when he asked, "Remember when we were in college, and we'd get dangerously close to losing control?"

She swallowed. "Yes."

"What did we do then?"

"We tried stupid distractions," she whispered, "like ice cream sundaes and jogs around the track."

"I don't want ice cream, and I'm too tired to jog. So what are we gonna do now?"

"I don't know," she whispered.

He pressed his forehead against hers and whispered, "I have an idea."

"What?"

"We could get married. Tonight. Surely there's a twenty-four-hour preacher around somewhere."

She smiled and reached up to touch the stubble on his jaw. "Are you proposing to me?"

His grin matched hers. "Depends. Would you accept if I did?"

Her smile faded slightly. "If I thought you were serious, I might consider considering it."

His eyes began to mist with emotion. "I am serious, Andi. In New York, I was more miserable than I've ever been, even though I was signing a deal for something I've worked years for. The thought that it wasn't a possibility that you would be a permanent part of my life . . . It was a little much to take . . ."

"Me, too," she whispered. "I was sick that it hadn't worked. That I had just been an obligation to you."

"Then let's stop playing games and do this thing right," he whispered. "Marry me, Andi."

She couldn't fight the tears streaming down her face. "There's nothing in the world I want more," she whispered.

"Tonight?" he asked.

"No. Not tonight. I want to do it right."

He looked a little helpless. "Then I guess it's time we went for a jog."

She smiled. "I'll get my running shoes."

Chapter Twenty-One

Cold arms of reality embraced Andi and Justin the next morning as they stood amid the ruins of Hands Across the Sea. An electrical flaw, the fireman's report had said when they'd finished their investigation this morning. The press was already having a field day with it, screaming that it was only a matter of time before something else started a fire. And what if there had been children inside, Givens was quoted as asking. To "save" the state from the horrors that could occur as a result of opening this park, he was taking action to make certain it remained closed.

"It'll be all right," Justin said from the destroyed entrance of the building. Andi stood in the center of the black, roofless structure, staring at the charred remains of her dream. Stepping over the sooty rubble, he slid his arms around her from the back. "It's just a setback."

Justin's touch reminded her that she was transparent, so she straightened her posture and forced a smile. "I know," she said, crossing her arms over his. "It'll be better when we rebuild it. We still have the plans, and the choreography for the automated figures is still composed on disk, so that's not entirely lost. It'll be fine." Her voice cracked with the last words, and she stepped out of his embrace. He watched her walk to one of the concrete sides and reach up to touch a melted mass of rubber that had been a child dressed in Dutch native dress. "I mean, I've overcome obstacles before," she said in a voice that lacked conviction. "This isn't going to get me down."

"Of course it won't," Justin said softly, wishing from his heart that he could make her discard that brave, positive facade and share her feelings with him. Stepping behind her again, he pulled her into his arms. For a moment she leaned her head against his broad shoulder in silent acceptance of his helping to carry the burden, but then, as if she thought better of it, she stiffened and stepped away again.

"Don't shut me out," Justin said.

Turning around, Andi tried to blink back her tears. "I'm not," she said, knowing her guard was slipping further with each passing moment and each gentle touch. "It's just that it's easier when no one understands how I feel. When everyone thinks I'm undaunted and ready to bounce back, I even believe it myself then."

"But I'm not everyone," he said.

"No, you're not," she agreed, swallowing back the tears blocking her throat. "And your understanding means ... everything. It's just that I don't have time to cry right now. There's too much to do, and I have to think." Her mouth trembled as she spoke, and the unshed tears blurred her eyes.

Justin set his hand on her shoulder, his face only inches from hers. Cupping her chin with his fingers, he ran a thumb over her bottom lip. "It's the press, isn't it? And that Givens maniac. You aren't afraid he'll carry out his threats to keep the park closed, are you?"

Andi heaved a deep sigh. "Justin, they aren't threats. He means it. He's been trying to close us down since the first groundbreaking."

"Why?" Justin asked, thinking it was despair talking rather than reason.

Andi bent down to pick up the metallic remains of a robot's hand. She fondled the smut-covered thing as if it were some personal object that brought back a memory. "Because this was his land before my father bought it, and he doesn't think we paid him enough for it."

"Well, he sold it to you, didn't he?"

Andi nodded. "Yes, and he got much more than it was worth. No one else would have ever bought it. It was all bayous, and he went through the whole deal as if he were getting away with something. But when he found out it was going to be the site of Promised Land, he felt he had been cheated."

"Why? Didn't he know who your father was?"

Andi shook her head. "He never saw him. My father had other men who scouted the area, and they in turn hired real estate agents to buy up all the land. None of them even knew who the buyer was. Dad knew that if word got out, the owners would jack the prices so high that it wouldn't even be feasible to put Promised Land here. It was perfectly legal, and he was fair with the prices he paid. But Givens owned most of it, and he thinks he was tricked somehow."

"Still," Justin said, "why would he deliberately set out to hurt Promised Land? That man owns a lot of the town. The revenues the park brings to this area could be worth a fortune to him."

Andi breathed a dry laugh. "It's gone beyond animosity, Justin. It's revenge now." Stepping closer to Justin, she glanced out the entrance to make certain that no one was listening. "After Dad's accident, he started rumors that Promised Land would fail without him. When he saw that I was going to prove him wrong, he approached me, insisting that I pay him an annual 'protection fee' to make sure that none of the townspeople set out to hurt Promised Land. I assured him that we could 'protect' ourselves."

Justin wasn't sure he understood. "Protection fee?" he asked. "Protection from whom? Givens himself?"

The question didn't require an answer. "I wasn't intimidated by his threats," Andi said. "I'm not big on being pushed around."

Justin almost smiled. "The man had a lot to learn about Andi Sherman, didn't he?"

"I thought so." She shrugged and looked around her, opening her arms helplessly. "But this is all he needs. This fire and the idea that it was an electrical problem are perfect ammunition for scaring the state into closing us down completely." Throwing down the metal hand, she raked her fingers through her hair in frazzled frustration. "Do you know what that would mean, Justin?" she asked, fresh emotion giving her haunted eyes new depth. "It would mean that I was ruined. There would be nothing left. Nothing. I put some of my Sherman Enterprises stock up as collateral to buy Promised Land stock when the investors wanted to pull out after Daddy's accident. And I used the rest to buy into your company because I believed in this park. I knew that I could see it through."

"You still believe in it," Justin said, his eyes intense. "I believe in it. You can do it, Andi. All you have to do is go and face the press. Answer their questions. Prove you have nothing to hide. By the time the park opens this will have died down and no one will even remember it."

Andi dropped her hands to her sides in helplessness. "You just don't understand, Justin," she whispered.

Justin wanted to hold her, but her stiffness and the wobbly edge in her voice warned him away. "I do understand," he said. "It seems like a terrible blow right now, but a few months from now it'll just be one more obstacle that you've overcome. You're a special woman, Andi, and I've seen you get around worse problems than this. It could have been so much worse. You might not have seen Madeline in time to save her. She would have died if she'd been in there a few minutes longer. And if we had gone in there just minutes later, the toxic fumes from the melted plastic might have killed us. But everyone's all right. We lost a building. Just a building, Andi! And God knows you've dealt with bad press before."

Knowing his words were steeped in truth, Andi heaved a long sigh and made her features relax. "I know you're right," she said. "I'll get through it. Give me an hour, and I'll be a pillar of strength. I always fall apart right at first, but my reconstruction usually makes me stronger." Setting her hands on her hips, she looked around her. "I'll call a press conference as soon as I meet with my animatronics engineers to discuss the rebuilding. And Press Preview Day is in just a few weeks. They'll see it firsthand and love it, even though all the rides aren't quite finished." She faltered, then took a deep breath. Walking into his outstretched arms and embracing him as if it were a way to absorb some of his strength, she said, "It's going to be all right, Justin. Now, I've got work to do."

"You go ahead," Justin said, hanging back. "I want to look around for a little while."

"All right," she said softly, pressing a kiss on his lips.

Justin watched her leave, noting the weary slump in her shoulders and her slow, hopeless gait. If only he could do more for her than offer her a strong embrace.

Kicking a charred beam out of his way, Justin walked to the back of the building where he remembered seeing Andi's silhouette against a wall of flames. His pulse raced anew as the picture snagged his mind, bringing back the fear that had screeched through him when he'd thought he had come too late. The fire had a better hold back there, he thought, and it seemed odd since the electrical work was only along the sides. Stepping closer, he kicked some of the debris from the fallen ceiling out of his way and found the place in the wall where an outlet had been. The firemen had chopped the area around it in their overhaul, leaving little evidence of the char patterns or melted aluminum. Something was wrong. Though the area around the outlet was still standing, it had burned to the ground just a few feet away. That was impossible if the fire had sprung from that outlet, for the point of origin was usually burned more thoroughly than any other area. Walking down the wall, he mentally measured the lowest level of burning. The wall had burned out in a V pattern with the lowest point almost in the center. That meant that the point of origin was probably just a few inches above the floor in a place where there had been no outlet. He'd have to check the blueprints when he got back to the office to make absolutely sure, but if he was right, the firemen who had done the investigation had been wrong. But what *had* started the fire?

Stepping over the wall into the bright sunlight that mocked such disaster, he looked at the back of the gutted building. This wall was the one that had sustained the most damage, for the other ones were still standing. Obviously it had not been the robots that had a defect in the wiring. Maybe it had been an extension cord plugged into the outlet and run along the length of the wall. Maybe the crew had walked on it so much that the wires had become bared and a fire started away from the outlet. But that was doubtful, since the construction had been finished in that part of the building and the robots had been hooked to their own electrical sources.

Brushing off his hands, Justin paced the length of the burned structure. Charred remains of the wall were scattered at his feet, and it seemed no clues had survived. Turning away from the building in frustration, he let his eyes sweep the ground.

An oblong pool of something white several yards from the debris caught his eye, and he walked toward it and stooped down for closer assessment. He ran his finger across it and realized that it was dried wax. Pulling his knife out of his pocket, Justin snapped out the blade and scraped up the dried substance until he came to an unburned wick stretched the length of it. *A melted candle,* he thought as a flash of lightning sparked something in his mind. In light of the fire and questionable point of origin, it seemed too much of a coincidence.

Closing his eyes, he strained to bring together fragments of memory—a criminal justice professor in college, a chapter on arson detection, a list of common methods. "One undetectable method," the professor had said, "is to soak the area in diesel fuel so that the fumes won't rise before the arsonist can get out of the building. He'll then set a candle in the middle of wadded paper, light it, and leave. By the time the candle burns out, the arsonist is gone, and the paper will catch fire, in turn setting off the fuel."

Could it be, Justin thought now, tracing the oblong circle of wax with his fingers, that the fire *was* the result of arson, and that the arsonist had dropped an extra candle on his way out of the building? Maybe Madeline had frightened the arsonist into making a careless escape.

Impossible, Justin thought, standing up. No one could have gotten onto the grounds without clearance, and the construction crews had gone home. There were no other signs of arson. At least none that he'd seen.

Running back over the rubble, Justin stepped over the wall and stood on the inside of the building again. Other clues to arson, he thought, racking his brain, were the smell of fumes in the charred wood. Picking up a piece that was charred less deeply than some of the others, he brought it to his nose. Nothing unusual. Moving the debris until he could reach the bottom layer that would have come from the wall instead of the ceiling, he picked up a more charred piece. Closing his eyes, he brought it to his nose, trying to block out the smell of burned wood and concentrate on any foreign vapor. His heart accelerated when the faintest smell of diesel fuel reached his nostrils. Ignoring the soot that coated his clothes, he began to clear away the debris closest to where he believed the fire had started. When he'd cleared a wide area, he peeled his shirt off his damp back and used it to sweep back the soot that blanketed the concrete.

A victorious smile captured his face as he found a line of char burned into the concrete in front of the lowest level of burning. Following the line on his hands and knees, continuously brushing the soot out of his way with his shirt, Justin saw that it led along the wall and toward the robots on both sides of the structure before it stopped. That was why the robots had not burned immediately. They had been free of the fire until the fuel-invoked flames had taken firm hold of the walls and spread toward the front of the building. And the center of the back wall had probably been splashed with diesel to ensure that the fire got a good start before the fire fighters could reach the scene.

Anticipation flooded through him as he stepped back over the shambles, realizing that all this combined evidence proved beyond a doubt that the fire was the result of arson. This would clear Promised Land of its responsibility. This would prove that it was not an electrical flaw that had caused the fire.

And it would give Andi back the drive and determination that had seemed wilting in her this morning. That alone was worth anything he could do.

In spite of her melancholy, Andi stifled a laugh when she saw Justin dart off the elevator covered with soot and perspiration, heading toward her office as if he had no time to waste.

"Justin," she called, hurrying across the reception area to meet him, noting the lull in typing and the surprised eyes that followed them into her office. "I was just coming from talking to Wes—"

"Arson," Justin cut in, his heavy breath diluting the impact of the word. "It was arson, Andi. Not some wiring problem. The fire was set deliberately."

Andi stood motionless, absorbing the meaning of his words. As the word took hold of her, confusion blurred her understanding. "But . . . the fire inspector said—"

"Forget what he said. It was arson. I can prove it." Justin started to lower himself to the ivory-colored sofa, then remembered he was covered with soot and caught himself. "My guess is that he used diesel to soak the wood of that back wall and the floor around it. Then he set a candle in the middle of paper or something and got out. He left one candle behind, so he must have heard someone coming before he could set up the second one. Probably Madeline."

"You found a candle? In all that debris, why didn't it melt?"

"I found it melted into the ground several yards behind the building." Remembering that piece of wood he'd saved, he pulled it from his pocket. "Smell this."

Andi inhaled and recognized the faint lacing of fumes. Bringing her alarmed eyes back to Justin, she asked, "Is this enough proof? Will the fire inspector determine it to be arson based on a smell and some melted wax?"

"We won't depend on him," Justin said, pacing back and forth in front of her. "If he overlooked this he's liable to overlook other things. This kind of thing is easy to miss if you're convinced something else was the problem. We'll call the arson squad. They'll know what else to look for. I also found a definite char pattern burned into the concrete. That's indisputable proof that an accelerant was poured onto the floor. You're clear, Andi. All we have to do is figure out who set it, have him arrested, and call a press conference. And then things can get back to normal around here."

Andi stood up and stopped Justin's pacing by stepping in front of him. Her eyes glowed with a moist rush of relief, and without thinking about the soot or dirt or how her clothes would look afterward, she reached up and wrapped her arms around his neck, embracing him with the strength of all the fear and dread she'd been experiencing since she'd read the headlines that morning. His dusty arms closed around her, crushing her against him with desperate tenderness.

"I told you we could get through it," he whispered into her hair as her warm tears wet his neck and twisted his heart, invoking the fiercest protection toward her, along with the love that multiplied with each passing day.

Chapter Twenty-Two

It was late afternoon before Andi and Justin, who had both showered and changed clothes, made it back to her office with the security tapes of yesterday's activities at each entrance to the park. They had convinced the arson squad that a mistake had been made in determining the cause of the fire, and now they were determined to find the culprit, even if it meant questioning everyone who had been on the grounds that day. They watched the tapes on her six screens, running them at a faster-than-normal speed, stopping the tapes every few minutes to determine who each person was and whether he had been an employee, crew member, or visitor.

"From now on the guards should write down everyone who comes in and out," Justin said wearily after they had been at it for several hours, "in case this ever comes up again."

Andi shook her head in disagreement. "They have a list of people who have clearance each day, and in the case of a visitor, they follow it up with a phone call. But too many people come in and out to write them all down, and it'll be worse when the park opens."

"Well, I don't want to have to do this again," Justin said, rubbing his hands down his tired face and sighing. "There's got to be a better way."

Andi smiled and looked over at him leaning back in his chair, an ankle slung over his knee.

"You know, you've gone way beyond the call of duty today," she said softly. "You've completely ignored your own work, and you don't have to."

"My staff is running things pretty smoothly," he said, taking her hand. "At this point, I'm not even sure we can trust your security guards to do this. It's too important, and I want to help."

"You have helped."

"I want to do more," he said, his eyes still on the screens. "I've come to like this park a lot, and I don't like the thought of some maniac out there who wants to mess it up. The next time we might not be so lucky."

Andi inclined her head and sighed. "A few weeks ago you wouldn't have lifted a finger for Promised Land. Or me."

Justin massaged the soft lines of her hand, fitted so naturally in his. "A few weeks ago I was a proud fool, still running from emotions so strong that they'd chased me for eight years."

His easy admission startled Andi, and she swallowed back the emotion constricting her throat. "And now?"

His eyes were the deepest shade of blue, dark as the night sky, as they smiled at her. "And now I've come to terms with those feelings." He brought her hand to his mouth, bent down, and kissed a knuckle. "I'm not going to run from them again." His voice was soft, velvety deep, indolent as he spoke. "I used to be so afraid of failing you somehow. You saw things in me that I couldn't even see in myself. But now I realize that I was never better than when I was with you. God knew it, too. That's why he brought us back together. And it doesn't scare me anymore."

Andi's eyes brimmed with emotion, and silent prayers of gratitude sang through her mind at the wonder of being in love. Tearing his eloquent eyes away from Andi's, Justin looked back at the screens.

"Looks like we're nearing the end of the workday," he said, breaking the spell and reluctantly dragging her attention back to the tapes. "Some of the crews are leaving right here. Slow them down a little." Picking up the list he and Andi had been compiling of people who'd come in during the day, they began to identify each person and check off the names as they went out.

When the activity at the entrances trickled down to one or two people coming through every few minutes, Justin glanced back over his list in search of a particular name. "You know who hasn't come out yet?"

"Who?" Andi asked, keeping her eyes on the screens.

"That building inspector who came in during the afternoon. Blond hair. Black pants and shirt."

Andi flipped back to an earlier page on her clipboard. "Butler's his name," she said. "Speed it up a little. Let's see if he came out late."

Justin set all the tapes on high speed, carefully watching for the man in question. When even two of the animators who had been with him until late into the night were shown exiting beneath the bright lights of the gates, he gave up. "That guy never came back out last night." The speeding tapes showed nothing for a few minutes, until the guard ran to open the gates to let the fire trucks in.

"Are you sure we didn't miss him?" Rewinding the tape, Andi searched the crowds who had left together at the end of the day.

Justin sat up straighter in his chair. "We didn't miss him." His eyes lit up as he looked askance at Andi. "Ten to one he had two candles and a can of diesel in that briefcase of his."

With great hope, Andi picked up the phone and dialed her head security guard. After ordering the tapes of the activities recorded so far today, she sat back and looked at the screens again. "If he went back out this morning," she said thoughtfully, "I think we've got our man."

"Had to," Justin said. "There's no other way out."

The hunch proved to be right. When they ran the tapes of that morning, they finally saw the building inspector hurrying out in the midst of a crew leaving the grounds for lunch. The first thing they did was report the man—Charles Butler of Shreveport—to the arson squad. The second thing was to call a press conference for the following day to clear the public's mind once and for all.

Chapter Twenty-Three

With the Press Preview Day still three weeks away, Andi invited the families of all of the Promised Land employees to have their run of the park, to test the rides and sleep in the hotels and sample the food, as a practice run for the employees and to offer any suggestions for last-minute improvements.

Andi and Justin tried to experience things as spectators rather than creators. They followed Wes and Laney around as Laney pushed the stroller with the new baby, and Justin rode some of the rides with Amy, listening to her squeal with laughter and beg for more turns. After a while, Madeline joined them, and Andi began to realize that the woman was someone she would like to have as a friend.

When Sherry Grayson, Wes's sister, showed up, she had more important things than the amusement park on her mind. She wore no make-up, as she usually did, and looked as though she'd been crying. "Wes, I've been trying to call you all night," she said.

"We stayed in one of the hotels on the grounds last night," he said. "What's wrong?"

"He's gone," she said. "Clint ... he's disappeared. I couldn't get in touch with him the night before last, or all day yesterday, and he just didn't show up at work, and no one knows where he is. The police won't consider him a missing person yet, but I've been in his house and he didn't take anything with him. Something's happened. People don't just disappear."

Andi couldn't help remembering that week that Justin had disappeared so long ago. That week when she had been lied to by her father; that week when she had reacted in a way that drove Justin away when he returned. And she couldn't forget the man who had stood next to her at the hospital nursery window, talking about the family he and Sherry would share. He was a man who believed in commitment, not one who would run from fear of responsibility. "Sherry, did he say anything about leaving? Does he have relatives who might have gotten sick? Was he upset?"

"No!" she cried. "Our wedding's in two weeks. He was helping me pack my stuff. I'm giving up my apartment at the end of the month, and we were starting to move some of my stuff over. He was as excited as I was. We were talking about children, how many we would have . . ." She broke into a sob and covered her face with both hands. "Wes, something's happened to him. I don't know what to do!"

"I'm sure there's an explanation," Laney said. "Try not to overreact."

"How can I not overreact?"

"You're not overreacting," Madeline said. "I'd be screaming if I were you." She hugged the girl, so easily, so naturally, that Andi envied it.

Andi didn't give hugs that easily—not to people she barely knew. But she had experience to give. "Sherry, about eight years ago, when Justin and I were seeing each other, he disappeared for a week. I believed that he had taken money to leave me. It turned out later that he just had to think for a few days, but he came back. By the time he did, I was worked into a rage, and I accused him of leaving me for money. It broke us up, and I've regretted it ever since."

Justin looked at her, and she knew that he was surprised that she would share so openly with them, when her privacy had been so important to her before.

"You can't overreact," she continued. "You have to trust. Trust God to be taking care of him. Trust Clint to do the right thing."

"I do trust him! But what if he's dead somewhere? What if he's had an accident, and he can't get help?"

"Was his car there?"

"No. It was gone, but other things were left. Clothes, shoes, his shaving kit... like he left in a big hurry, or intended to come back. Wes, will you please come to the police station with me? Convince them to take this seriously? They think it was cold feet, that he made a quick escape before he had to tie the knot. Please, Wes. They'll listen to you!"

"All right, Sis," he said. "Laney, will you be all right?"

"With a little help," Laney said, grinning around at those with her.

"I'll help!" Madeline offered. "In fact, if the baby gets too hot, I can take him up to my office and let him sleep for a while. I'd love to."

"I would, too," Andi said. "Between Madeline, Justin, and me, we can help you out."

"Fine, then. Go," Laney said to Wes. "Sherry, I know things are going to be all right. Clint's not the kind of man to disappear without a reason."

"Not unless he didn't have a choice," Sherry said.

But a week later, he still wasn't back, and Sherry had gotten no more satisfaction. The police department did consider him a missing person now, but they had no leads on where he may have gone, how he would have gotten there, why he wouldn't have taken clothes ... She reported it to the television station, and they put his picture on the evening news and asked for information concerning his whereabouts.

Days went by, however, and there was no word. The police attributed his disappearance to cold feet, and stopped looking. Their blasé attitude devastated Sherry—but soon she began to wonder, herself. Finally, when the day came to move out of her apartment, Madeline saved the day. "Sherry, I just bought that big house, and I would love for you to come stay with me, and then when Clint gets back, you won't be tied down with a lease and stuff. It's no Taj Mahal, but it's a nice house. And we'll have fun, just us girls. Come on, what do you say?"

Reluctantly, Sherry agreed, and the whole group helped her move. Andi began to feel a part of this circle of friends, something she hadn't felt since college, and she felt as if she contributed something. Even though the preview day was nearing, this personal crisis seemed to be even more immediate, more important.

Speculation grew about Clint's disappearance, and those who loved him worried themselves sick. But Andi had a feeling that they would hear from him again. It was a lesson she had learned the hard way. She just hoped that Sherry would handle it better than she had when he finally did return.

Chapter Twenty-Four

The Louisiana sun was on stage the day of the preview, glowing hot and magnificent in a cobalt sky. Though Hands Across the Sea had not yet been rebuilt, most of the rides were operative after grueling weeks of around-the-clock work, and more than two hundred fifty press people had been flown in for a firsthand impression of the phenomenon that was Promised Land. From the lifelike performances of ancient Bible characters in the Hall of Faith to the whale rides that took people to the underwater city, the magic followed the visitors, enchanting and delighting them more with each step. Even the unfinished rides were toured so that the media could get some idea of the fantasies yet to be tapped. And Downtown, Planet Earth, the main strip of shops through the rides, captivated everyone with souvenirs and toys of the soon-to-be-famous cartoon characters who romped the park in costume, stopping to pose for snapshots between shenanigans especially choreographed and rehearsed to look spontaneous. Live music provided the transitions from one theme area to the next, and every three hours a parade with all the Promised Land characters and the special uniformed praise band danced down the winding maze of sidewalks.

Andi seemed to be everywhere at once, making certain that her trained employees had no problems and ironing out last-minute mini-catastrophes as they presented themselves. It was working, she thought with a slight shiver, though the midafternoon sun blazed onto her tanned skin. The press people were enthralled, and by tomorrow the whole world would be buzzing with talk about this special kingdom.

Leaning on the rail of the bridge that arched over the "ocean," Andi watched the robotic whales disappear beneath her. A feeling of bursting delight rose within her as she anticipated that group's reaction when they saw the aqua magic. There were few things more gratifying than taking an idea and turning it into something that other people could see. She would have given anything to have her father beside her to experience it. She thanked God she had Justin.

"Excuse me," a deep voice said in her ear as two strong arms slipped around her waist. "Are you one of the clones of Andi Sherman that have been running around here, or the real thing?" Andi smiled and caught her breath as Justin dipped his head and nuzzled her neck. "Mmmm. Has to be the real thing," he murmured in a lazy voice.

Andi leaned back against his chest. "Sounds like a good idea, though," she sighed. "Maybe we could have a few robots made up of me to take care of some of the minor problems around here."

Justin's deep laughter vibrated through her. "You'd be bored stiff. Besides, there's no way they could capture that spirit of yours in a bundle of machinery."

It was Andi's turn to laugh. "I don't know how to take that."

Justin stepped to her side and braced himself on the rail as he grinned wryly. "I wouldn't take orders from a robot."

Andi gave a dry laugh. "You don't take orders from me."

Justin shrugged. "But it's a lot more fun saying no to you than it would be to a robot." Tipping her chin up, he grinned down at her.

Andi reached up to trace his bottom lip with her fingertip.

Taking her hand in both of his, he fondled it, running his thumb along the palm, creating a stirring sensation that heated her blood. "I've always known you were something special," he said in a husky voice as a gust of wind swept back her long curls. "But today, I've decided you're a genius."

Andi smiled and gave a slight shrug. "No genius," she said. "I just have a lot of faith."

Justin took in the view around him as he continued holding her hand. "But that kind of faith isn't always easy."

Andi was uncomfortable with such bold praise and shrugged it off again. "I had a lot of help."

"But they were your dreams. God gave them to you, and you had the boldness to carry them out."

"Mine and Dad's." Her limpid green eyes sparkled as they swept over the jutting, colorful buildings and listened to the delightful laughter of overworked journalists who were clearly enjoying themselves. A bell rang in the distance, warning that the FanTran was about to make its first test run of the day, though no passengers were aboard due to the unfinished tunnels it threaded through.

"I never understood that about you when we were together in college," Justin went on softly, setting her hand on the rail and leaning next to her on his elbows. His voice drew her into a different dimension. "I used to think that your dreams and your striving to make them come true was just a characteristic of someone who'd always gotten everything she wanted. But it isn't so."

Andi dropped her eyes to her hands smoothing over the finely sanded wood. "No, it isn't."

"It took me all this time to realize that your dream is a measure of your potential. That sparkle in your eye means that big things are going to happen. That God has a special plan."

Andi breathed out a long sigh and smiled over at him. "Is this a brand-new observation?"

"No," he said softly. "It's an exaltation. I'm going to marry a woman with dreams as big as I have."

Andi touched his face and, looking up into eyes that could always embrace her heart, she smiled.

Justin slid his arms around her waist and pulled her closer as the FanTran picked up speed on the curve over the Jonah ride. "So, when are you gonna marry me? I've waited patiently while we got ready for Press Day. But we should really make an announcement today. Just to top things off."

Excitement filled her eyes. "All right. Why don't we tell them we're getting married on Opening Day? We'll have the ceremony right here in the park."

"I love it," he said. "I love you . . ."

A deafening crash cut off his words, vibrating thunder with all the sound and fury of an earthquake, tearing their attention to the unfinished side of the park.

"The FanTran!" someone shouted, and Andi began to run blindly, like a mother running to move her child from the path of a speeding car, but when she reached the accident, she saw that it was too late. The train had jumped the track and crashed headfirst into one of the unfinished buildings below it, but its caboose and long center cars still inched along the rails, slowly promising a second crash that would destroy at least two other buildings.

"Get back!" Andi shouted as the spectators around her froze for a soundless eternity, bracing themselves for the second fall as if their very breath could be the catalyst that sent it hurling to the ground. When the caboose at last let go, it seemed to fall in a slow-motion dance, mocking the helplessness of those who cared, as the train crashed into crumbling roofs in ruinous defiance of the dreams beneath them.

Chapter Twenty-Five

Andi sat curled on the corner of her bedroom windowsill, watching the progress of two robins constructing a nest with fluttering diligence in a tree below her window. From the doorway, Justin watched her, wondering why they absorbed her attention so completely. Did they provide a sort of mental anesthesia that prevented her from glancing beyond the tree to the sight of the cranes struggling to pull the FanTran from the wreckage? The press was having a field day, reporting "on-the-scene" coverage of the disaster that could have taken hundreds of lives had the park been open to the public. There was speculation that the problems with the FanTran had been the reason that Andi had not let the visitors ride it, but that her "gambling" nature had caused her to take the chance and let it run anyway.

But she wasn't watching the wreckage. She was concentrating on watching the birds, as if seeing some other creature building something worthwhile would enable her to hold herself together for a while longer.

Justin went into her bedroom, a glass of water in one hand and two aspirin in the other. "Take these," he ordered, dropping them into her hand. "It'll help your headache." She took the aspirin gratefully and drank by rote.

"Are you okay?" Justin asked, his deep, probing voice piercing her cocoon of irrelevant thoughts.

"Fine," she said, slipping away before he could touch her. Guardedly, she folded her arms across her stomach as her psyche threatened to crumble.

Justin watched Andi bring the glass to her lips again, the water sloshing dangerously with the movement of her trembling hands. Her hair, though rumpled from her fingers pushing absently through it, was still curled and shining over her shoulders, and the light overhead gave it the dazzling effect of burnished golden threads that had never seen dark days. But her jade eyes were haunted and hiding, and her face was pale, reflecting the turmoil within her that he had no idea how to calm.

"It'll be all right," he said softly, helplessly. "It might delay the opening a couple of months, but—"

"There isn't going to be an opening," Andi said in a hopeless monotone. "Promised Land is going to be an enormous white elephant. Even if I had the money to rebuild, which I don't, no one in his right mind would risk coming here now."

Rolling up his cuffs to busy his hands, Justin tried again. "I know it seems bad right now. But you've got to fight back. You can't let a thing like this get you down."

His unconvincing pep talk struck her as funny, but her laughter did not hide the gravity beneath it. "A thing like this?" She leaned toward him as if the stance would help to make her point. "Justin, the earth might as well have crumbled underneath us and swallowed the whole park. It's over. I should have seen it a long time ago. It's not genius you've been seeing in me—it's stupidity! None of this was God's plan. I misread him. It was *my* plan." Her eyes filled with angry tears and she struggled against them, covering her face with her hands.

Swallowing back his own emotion at her pain, Justin took her by the arms and forced her to look at him. Her face was raging red as she dropped her hands and clutched his forearms as if they could anchor her. "It was not stupid," he said. "You saw those people out there today. They loved Promised Land, and you know it."

"Sure," Andi cried, glaring up at him, desperately in need of someone to bear the daggers of her anger. "They loved it! They're still loving it! Look at them out there with their camera crews and microphones. Everybody loves a good horror! Too bad you can only give the show once!"

"No one was hurt, Andi!"

"But what about next time?" she railed. "How many people will be killed in the next disaster? Even if the public could forget about all this, *I* never will!" She slammed the glass down and turned around, trying to find the words she needed. "I tried to watch everything. Make sure that nothing went wrong. I inspected everything over and over. But I can't know everything, and I can't be everywhere!"

Justin tucked her against him, though she struggled to pull away, and held her still until her racking, furious sobs calmed a few degrees. There were no answers. He had no great morsel of wisdom to offer, no burst of inspiration that would see her through this. The realization of his inadequacies left him furious at himself.

"You've been through a lot," he whispered, rocking her back and forth as her body relaxed into him.

Andi nodded. "I should have given up when Dad had his accident. Everyone warned me to. I could have gotten out and no one would have blamed me. I should have known I couldn't *be* him. This would never have happened if he'd been running things. But I just wanted him to be proud of me when he came to! So I hung on, faking my way through all of it, pretending, even to myself, that I could do anything."

"You *can* do anything," he said with deepest certainty, pulling her down to sit next to him on the small love seat against the wall. "But you couldn't have stopped this. You're one person. I've never seen a president of a company so involved on every level. Your father was proud of you and he knew you were as capable as he was, or he would never have left you in charge."

His words seemed to relax her more, so he closed his arms more tightly around her and went on in his deep, comforting baritone, realizing she needed the truth, realizing she needed his love. "That's probably why he fought our relationship so hard. He knew you were too good for me. He knew I was just a lousy bum who didn't appreciate what a precious treasure you were. And at the time, he was right."

The memory of her father's love for her racked her even deeper, and she wept into his chest, clutching the edge of his shirt as she groped for some means of control.

"Tell me what your father would have done differently to prevent today's accident," Justin prodded.

"I don't know," she cried in a strained voice. "But he would have known. He knew so much more than I did. I overlooked something. I ignored something."

"Wrong," Justin said, pulling her back so that he could see her wild, red-rimmed eyes. "Even the engineers who designed the FanTran didn't see it. You said yourself you have some of the best minds in the world working for you. It'll be okay. You can rebuild these rides, perfect the FanTran ... We'll think of a way to clear our image."

"There's no time," Andi said in a hoarse voice. "The country's going to get tired of these conflicting signals. We'd have to suffer through months, maybe years, of no profits at all before people started to come. And I can't rebuild these rides. There was too much damage. I've made a mockery out of the whole idea that this was a God-centered park."

"You haven't made it a mockery. You're rebuilding Hands Across the Sea, aren't you?"

Andi pulled out of his arms and stood up. "You don't understand, Justin. I'm not talking about construction capabilities and the strength of a dream. I'm talking about money. I simply don't have the money if the park isn't going to open! I only have enough to get us through construction and the first year until we start seeing a profit. But no one will come now. There won't be any profits, and there's no more in the budget for rebuilding."

"You can borrow it. Surely—"

"I can't borrow any more," she bit out, turning back to him. "I told you. I've used all my Sherman Enterprises stock as collateral for the loans I've already gotten. There's very little left, and no bank in the world is going to loan me money after this. I won't be able to pay it back. I'm going bankrupt, Justin. There's no other alternative."

"Yes, there is," Justin demurred with a gentle shake of her arm. "You still have half of Pierce Productions. My company is worth a lot more now than it was. And if your fifty percent isn't enough collateral, I could borrow on my half and help."

"I'd never let you do that," she whispered, turning away from him. "This is not your problem, it's mine."

"You're going to be my wife." He forced her to face him again. "That makes it my problem."

Andi couldn't stop the peal of laughter bursting through her sobs. "Your wife? I can't marry you now!"

Not willing to accept a decision made during hysteria, Justin framed her face and tipped it up to his. "Yes, you can. This thing today has nothing to do with us or our future together."

"It does," she cried. "Don't you see? I can't marry you now. I have nothing left. Nothing!"

"You have me! And we both have Pierce Productions. I'll help you through this."

"You're always helping me through catastrophes lately, Justin!" she shouted in a frazzled pitch. "I can't go through life leaning on you!"

"I like for you to lean on me," he said earnestly. "That's why God wants us to have helpmeets. So we can help each other."

"But I can't, Justin!" Her face burned hot with conviction. "That's why we never made it before. I had money, big ideas, and big dreams. I had energy and drive, and it made you crazy. If I had been poor and ordinary we might have stayed together. It's no wonder that you want me now. You've got me right where you've always wanted me!"

Justin turned to the dresser, leaning on his hands, and forced his eyes on the forgotten glass of water. "I never said I wanted you to be those things," he bit out in a tremulous voice, trying to keep her condition in mind. "I asked you to marry me *before* the FanTran crashed. I told you that I understood my mistakes. I love you just the way you are, Andi. Don't ruin it."

Andi's fingernails bit into her palms as she brought her fists to her temples. "You can't love me the way I am when I don't even *know* who I am anymore. I just know I can't start off a marriage trying to find myself, trying to pick up the pieces and patch things back together." She stopped and looked at him, his back to her, his muscles coiled and poised for the coming blow. "It won't work, Justin," she said, trying to keep the despair from her voice. "I'm not going to marry you."

The glass beside his hand went flying across the room. It crashed on the wall and splintered to the floor, leaving behind it only a dripping wet stain on the wallpaper. "Give it up, then!" he blared as Andi turned her back to him and muffled her sob with her fists. "It's you who has to have everything perfect, Andi. You're fine as long as you're in control, as long as you're the one with the money and the strings and the ideas. But lose a few notches on that pedestal of yours, and everybody else had better look out. You'd rather go under than accept my help, wouldn't you? You'd rather live alone the rest of your life than marry someone who wants to protect you." His voice softened with emotion as he stepped up behind her, the warmth of his body radiating into her, though he refrained from touching her. "That first day I came to your office to hear your proposal, you told me that it was always easier to settle for something instead of fighting and trying to make it work. You were right." His hands touched the backs of her shoulders and he dropped his forehead into her hair. "Marry me, Andi," he pleaded in a tremulous voice. "We can make it. If we throw it out this time, we'll never get it back. It'll be lost to us forever."

"It's already lost," she whispered.

Justin dropped his hands and stepped back, and she forced herself to stand still and not look at him. "As long as I've known you," he said in a flat, bland voice, "you've fought through every crisis in your life. But you won't fight for me. Well, maybe you don't consider losing me a crisis."

Silent, she stayed where she was, her back to him.

"That's right, Andi," Justin bit out. "Don't say anything. Let me just keep thinking that you still love me in your way. It'll help at night when I'm racking my brain trying to figure this insanity out." He started out of the room, his heart shattering like broken glass. "I love you anyway, Andi," he said in a strange, thick voice.

And then he was gone, leaving behind only a sick, throbbing void where hope had been.

It was two hours before Andi felt she had no more tears to shed, and then she forced herself to pull together and consider the steps that had to be taken. Like the preparations for a funeral, arrangements had to be made to put an end to Promised Land. Padding barefoot into her kitchen, Andi poured herself a drink, then reached into her freezer for a handful of ice cubes. Breathing a deep, cleansing sigh, she dropped all but two into her glass and pressed the two remaining ones against her swollen eyes. The park was gone, she thought, trying to get her priorities in order. There was no sense in mourning it anymore. She would do what had to be done and get it behind her as soon as possible.

The way she had done with Justin.

She thought of his offer to help her financially. The ironies of life would never cease to amaze her. They had completely switched positions. Now he was the one succeeding and executing dreams, and she would soon be penniless.

For the first time in her life she understood why he had been so resisting of her help before. It hurt to ask someone you loved for help. But it also hurt to want to help someone you loved and be denied that privilege. There was no winning between them. They were too much alike.

Berating herself for being as proud and stubborn as he had once been, she walked back to her bedroom window and saw the sun beginning to set in the west. The crowd of reporters still circled around the wreckage like vultures, waiting for any morsel of information they could glean. They were so fickle, she thought with misery. This morning they had been her hailing followers, and tonight they would do her in.

What are you trying to teach me, Lord? her mind cried out. *What is it that I'm not learning?*

Something about pride, she told herself. She had confessed it time and time again, had pleaded with God to change her, but here it was, still driving her. The memory of Justin's voice when he'd left her today, letting her know that she could still change her mind, rang through her heart. He did love her, and God knew she loved him. But was her pride really going to cost her everything? Wasn't she strong enough to keep from emotionally dragging him down if they stayed together?

Her eyes drifted to the telephone beside the red couch and she sat down and set her hand on the receiver. The smoothness of it almost made her feel better, so she picked it up. What would she say? That maybe they could make it? That her love for him was stronger than her pride? That it might be possible for Pierce Production's small initial income to get her park through the rough periods while she put off her debtors? That maybe she could delay bankruptcy until . . .

Pierce Productions. The words punctured her heart, sending the breath of hope whooshing out until there was none left. Pierce Productions was half owned by Promised Land. And if Promised Land was forced into bankruptcy, Pierce Productions would go down as well.

Andi dropped the phone back in its cradle. She had been wrong when she'd thought things could never get worse. They could get far worse.

She had only one choice. She would give Justin his fifty percent back. She would make certain that he was free and clear of Promised Land before she petitioned for bankruptcy. And she would make even more certain that their paths did not cross until the deed was done. That way there would be no turning back. She could not cling to Justin's dream in hopes it would save her own. The risk of stripping him of everything was too great.

If she could not save herself, she would at least save him. Again, she picked up the telephone. But this time she called her lawyers.

Chapter Twenty-Six

Andi buried her head in her arms, wrinkling the useless papers cluttering her desk. It felt as if every ounce of blood had been drained from her veins, and it was just too much to endure. Justin would get the papers today, cutting him loose from Promised Land. He would be angry at first, she thought dismally. But when her lawyer pointed out that he would probably lose his company otherwise, she was certain he'd understand. Justin had fought her control of him almost every step of the way, and now she was simply giving back what she had taken. When the papers were signed, she could go ahead with her petition for bankruptcy.

Then she would start over . . . somewhere.

Lord, how is this going to make me stronger? her mind railed. Her father's notes next to the "consider it joy" verse in his Bible came back to her, and she tried with all her heart and soul to find some joy in what was happening. But the truth was, she didn't care if it made her stronger to endure this. If that was the cost, she didn't want to be strong.

The door bolted open, startling her into lifting her head, and suddenly Justin stood before her, his explosive blue eyes burning into her as he slammed the door and stalked to her desk. Leaning over it, he shoved the crumpled paper across the desk top. "You always have the last word, don't you?"

Andi was stunned into speechlessness, but she opened her mouth and tried to reply.

"Well, swallow this," he blazed, cutting her off. "Promised Land is half owner of Pierce Productions. And it's going to stay that way. We're in this together, and whether you like it or not, we're going to fight it out together!"

Andi stood up and faced him at eye level, her red eyes tired and swollen. "Justin, you don't understand. I'm not trying to pull rank on you. I just don't want your company to be hurt."

"Forget my company!" he shouted. "It's not worth anything without you! *I'm* not worth anything without you. Why can't you understand that?"

Andi couldn't answer. Trying to hide her pain, she turned her back to him and leaned into one of the closed circuit television screens, busy with the forms of Givens and the state inspectors who had been in and out for the last two days, gathering ammunition to take back to the legislature to hurry her demise.

Anger seeped away from him as he saw a tear drop from her chin. He wanted to hold her, to forget either company had ever existed, to take her away somewhere where they could both start over with new dreams. He stepped around her desk, still keeping some distance between them and honoring her need to hide her face. "We can fight it together, Andi," he pleaded. "And if it comes to it, losing my company would be nothing compared to losing you."

She heard him moving toward her, and when his arms closed around her from the back, she thought how easy it would be to just turn to him and accept his love and his help. But it was the coward's way out. She had always been praised for her vision. And right now that vision was telling her that nothing was going to get better. If he lost his company because of her, deep down he would never forgive her and she would never forgive herself.

"But if we don't lose our companies, Andi, we'll be stronger together. You've got to get back on your feet if you're going to invest in my movie." His soft voice cut into her thoughts, drawing her upward again on the emotional seesaw she rode, as he diagrammed new dreams. "It'll be a masterpiece for children and adults, and they'll show it over and over for a hundred years."

Andi closed her eyes. "You wouldn't take the money for the film when I had it, Justin. It's easy to accept now when I don't have it. I appreciate the effort, but it's an empty gesture."

Justin stepped back and dropped his hands, his tone hinting at vexation and helplessness. "Right now you see everything I do as an empty gesture, Andi. I don't know how to convince you that I have no intentions of letting you or your dreams go."

Didn't he understand? Didn't he realize that the chances of their pulling out of this mess were next to nothing? Maybe his conscience wouldn't allow him to leave her behind when things were so rough, the way he had done before. She'd just have to make herself strong and show him that she could make it on her own. Somehow, she would have to convince him to forget her and save himself.

Walking to the window, Andi squared her shoulders. "Justin, part of being a dreamer has to do with knowing when to let go. There isn't going to be some miracle that turns things around this time. It just wasn't meant to be."

"Don't tell me about letting go!" he shouted. "I've had a lot more blows in my life than you have. Being a dreamer means holding on, working and sweating and praying until you see that dream taking shape. If I had let go every time the earth fell out from under me, I'd be in another galaxy by now. Your dad didn't make his millions giving up when things looked bad. He fought back. He made a lot of enemies that way, but he also built a lot of dreams. And he trusted, because he knew that God was in it!"

"He would have done the same thing I'm doing now!" Andi cried, swinging around to face Justin.

"I don't think so," he said, planting his hands on his hips as the pulse beat visibly in his neck. "He would have taken every advantage he had, and you know it."

Andi's face glowed with frustration. "Don't you understand?" she rasped. "I don't have any advantages right now!"

"You have me!" he shouted back. "We may not be millionaires when we come out of this, but we also will probably not be bankrupt! You're just too wrapped up in martyrdom to see it!"

Andi's heart pumped furiously. She would lose the battle and he would lose, unless she did something drastic. "It isn't martyrdom, Justin," she cried. "It's just that the last thing you do before your ship sinks is throw the deadweight overboard. It'll be months before you show a profit. I want out, Justin. When I'm rid of you I can concentrate on my own interests."

Justin looked as if he had been struck across the face. He froze, speechless, for a tortuous eternity, his lips a tight slash across his face, his jaws visibly clenched. Slowly, he turned back to her desk and retrieved the paper. She watched the hard way he swallowed as he stared down at it, as if battling the decision that only needed a signature. And when he finally brought his eyes to her again, she saw that the pain had been replaced with something hotter and more vibrant. "We've bluffed each other before, Andi," he said in a quiet, lethal voice. "But the stakes are a lot higher this time." He started toward the door, opened it, but stopped at the threshold and turned back to her. His blue eyes were luminous with new purpose when he held up the paper and ripped it in half.

Andi caught her breath and started forward to stop him, but he warned her back with an outstretched hand. "We're going down together, Andi, or we'll fight it out together," he seethed, his voice tremulously quiet as he continued to shred the paper, letting the pieces float to the floor. "And when it's all over, regardless of the outcome, we'll have something more important than any of it left."

Then he disappeared, slamming the door behind him, leaving only a scattered pile of paper that represented the hope that Andi was afraid to feel.

Justin's hands still trembled with anger as he rode the glass elevator down to the first floor. Deadweight. He knew her words were only an attempt to shock him into signing her papers, but they still rankled him. He'd show her deadweight. And when he did, she would be begging *him* for a trip to the altar.

"It's an awesome responsibility being so blasted sure of yourself, Pierce," Justin said aloud as he stormed across the lobby and out onto the Promised Land grounds. The cool air ruffled his hair, but did nothing to cool his temper. What if it wasn't a bluff? What if those papers really were her attempt to rid herself of the extra weight while she fought against her own demise? If she had never bought Pierce Productions, she might not be in so much financial trouble. But the irony of it was that if the park were going to open as scheduled, she would still be a wealthy woman and the amount of money she had paid him for half of his company wouldn't have even put a dent in her bank account. It was the threat of nervous stockholders that would do her in. If he could just convince them to give her some time to make the park work. If he could just convince *her* to try.

He jammed his hands into his pockets and started toward the wreckage, desperately racking his brain for some way to give her back her hope. He understood futility because he'd felt it many times himself. They were two of a kind, he and Andi, and neither of them could survive on someone else's good graces. But if he could give her back some of what she had lost—if he could find a way to salvage the park's reputation . . . Maybe they could put the harsh words and cruelties behind them and just move forward with their dreams.

Rounding the Noah's Ark section of the park, Justin could see the work crews still laboring to clear the rubble out of the smashed buildings. The wrecked FanTran cars had been removed and were crumpled between two buildings, and the thick tracks hung from the broken bridge, as if waiting for someone to come along to put them back together. *You can do it, Lord,* he prayed silently. *You can put it all back together. You can show us how to.*

Helpless, he racked his brain for what could have gone wrong. How could Andi's engineers have made such a colossal error? The FanTran had been on hundreds of test runs, and there had never even been the hint of a snag in the tracks before. How could they have just worked loose so suddenly? Why would it have happened on that day, of all days?

Walking through the workers and the civil engineers with their clipboards and reports, Justin went to the site where the first car had fallen and kicked aside the splintered beams.

Jeanine Calaveras, the anchorwoman he had met at the press party, came up behind him with her live camera and sound crew. "Mr. Pierce," she said, taking him by the arm and turning him to face the camera. "How is this disaster going to affect Pierce Productions?"

Moving his arm out of her grasp, Justin took an evasive step backward. "The same way it affects Promised Land," he said, starting to walk away.

But the crew followed him. "Mr. Pierce, do you regret selling your company to Miss Sherman?"

Justin stopped, keeping his back to the reporter and her camera. "No, I do not."

"Will this affect your relationship with Miss Sherman in any way? Rumor had it that the two of you were becoming involved again."

Justin set his hands on his hips and turned to face the probing woman. "What is it, a slow day? No murders? No wars? Is my love life really that interesting to you?"

Squaring her shoulders, Jeanine gave a flick of her fingers telling her cameraman to stop rolling. "He's not going to give us anything," she told her crew. "Why don't we go ask Andi herself?"

Justin's granite features were cold and unyielding, and his eyes gave warnings that no one with any intelligence would have challenged. "You get within forty feet of her and I'll have you arrested for harassment. You're already trespassing."

Jeanine shrugged. "Security has been a bit lax since the crash. I guess they figure 'what's the use?'"

Justin raked his hands through his hair, desperately trying to keep calm. "You know, Miss Calaveras," he said in a dangerously unaffected tone, "I've had a rough day. The kind of day that makes me want to smash someone's face in. I'm not accustomed to hitting women, but shattering those cameras of yours might let off a little of my frustration."

"Are you threatening me?" the woman asked in a haughty voice, though she stepped back.

Justin gazed down at her for a moment, a slow, agitated grin curling his lips. "That's exactly what I'm doing," he said, then walked away.

A group of men a few feet away caught his attention. Another reporter was interviewing them about their "expert opinions" on the crash. Givens was among them. "It's simply what I've been warning the state about for months. When the legislature takes away a parish's right to govern something within its boundaries, they're asking for trouble. If we had been involved in this, the accident would never have happened."

"But, Mr. Givens," the reporter prodded, "isn't it true that the parish was gratuitously involved in inspecting each structure?"

The man shrugged his massive shoulders, clasping his hands over his belly. "Yes, that's true. But our building inspectors' suggestions were usually ignored. We had no means of enforcing anything we saw. In this case they obviously used lower-grade materials, did a haphazard job of bolting—"

Unable to stand another word, Justin changed directions and saw Wes sitting off to the side on a crate, his chin propped on a fist. Picking up one of the heavy broken beams, Justin went to sit beside him. "What do you think?" he asked.

Wes shook his head helplessly. "It was not lower grade," he said in a voice too low for anyone else to hear. "And the bolting was done with an air compressor. I checked them myself." He slid his hands down his face and looked at the wreckage over his fingertips. "I was here every step of the way. So were the other engineers. When anything looked even questionable, we started over. We don't do shoddy work. Those tracks were stable."

Justin stood up and surveyed the broken tracks overhead, then brought his eyes down to Wes. "Then how do you explain what happened?"

With bloodshot eyes, his friend looked up at the tracks still hanging from the sagging bridge. "If it was what they're saying, we would have noticed it. It wouldn't have jumped like that. Even a loose track wouldn't have worked completely free that fast. And I would have noticed it yesterday morning when I ran the detector car around. It would have picked up any flaw in the rails. But there was nothing." Wearily, he rubbed his hands across his jaws. "I can't help wondering if I missed something. I've been a little tired with the new baby and Clint's disappearance and Sherry's depression and all . . . what if there was something I should have checked, something that could have prevented all this? I just can't think what it would be."

"You're not the engineer, Wes. There's nothing you could have done."

"It just doesn't make sense. It ran so smoothly."

Justin moved his thumb along the bare spot of his chest, a frown working at his brows as he looked at the bent rails. "Do you think someone could have deliberately done this? We've established that the fire was arson. Maybe somebody was trying to finish the job of sabotaging the park. This would be a terrific way to do it. It worked."

Wes brought tired, troubled eyes to Justin's. He opened his mouth to speak, then glanced around him to make certain no one could hear. "I can't prove a thing," he muttered.

A new sense of purpose fell over Justin as suspicion filled his heart. Why hadn't he thought of it before? Forgetting Wes, Justin stood up and walked the length of the trestle until it sloped to the ground enough for him to climb up on it. Then he walked back up the tracks, studying each cross tie for any clue, until he stood above Wes. Kneeling down, he ran his hand along the rails, praying he would find something, anything. A state engineer ran up the tracks behind him, holding his clipboard under his arm as he glared down at Justin. "May I ask what you're doing, sir?"

"Examining the rails," Justin clipped without ceasing his work.

The man stepped closer to hinder Justin's progress. "For what?"

"For anything," Justin said.

"I've already examined them and made my report," he said. "There's no need—"

"Get out of my way!" Justin bellowed as he ran his fingers over the holes of the tie plates where the spikes had come loose.

The man became more ruffled. "If you don't stop right this minute, I'll have you forcefully removed from the premises. You're getting in the way of an investigation."

"Fine," Justin mumbled, glancing up at the man with imposing, daggerlike eyes. "You just try it."

Catching an exasperated, agitated breath, the man hurried away, presumably to get help. But Justin still wasn't daunted. "There's not a bolt left in place here, Wes. Not on either rail for about twenty feet." He leaned forward to an almost hanging position until he could see the end of the twisted piece of rail. "Did you notice that one of the joint bars is missing?"

Wes shook his head sadly. "We checked every bolt. I walked these tracks myself, just the other day."

As if he hadn't heard, Justin studied the twist of the rails, battered on the ends and bent, as if some outside force had pried the ends up enough to ensure their instability. He got up and walked back up the tracks, racking his brain for an answer. He looked around for a camera from which the security guards could monitor the rails. If someone had sneaked in, as they'd done the other night to start the fire, and had deliberately damaged the tracks, wouldn't it be recorded? Wouldn't they be able to replay the tapes and see if someone was there?

He leapt down and headed to the security guards' station. "I need to see the tapes monitoring the damaged section of the FanTran rails," he told the guards sitting at the closed circuit televisions. "All the tapes just prior to the accident."

One of the guards, an elderly man who looked like someone's grandpa, got up and went to the tape room at the back of the small building. "Let's see," he said as they found the tapes of that edge of the park. "Here are the cameras monitoring the Noah's Ark ride, and part of that track is visible from that camera. But now that I think about it, it's not the part that was damaged. It's just the part before it curves around ..."

Justin took the tape and popped it in the VCR at the corner of the room. "Sure is. It just misses the section I need to see. What else you got?"

"Well ... there's the Jacob's Ladder section. It might show some of that track, but from a distance." He took the tape out and popped the new one in. The track was too far above the picture. "Nope. That doesn't show it."

Justin couldn't believe it. "Do you mean to tell me that we don't have cameras monitoring every part of the FanTran track?"

"No, sir. You see, the cameras are to monitor people. And it isn't likely that people will be on those tracks. So the cameras aren't on them ... not specifically."

"So there's no way to see if someone walked those tracks and damaged them?"

"No, sir. But we can do like you did the other day, when you checked the tapes of those who came in and out."

"That'll never work this time," Justin said. "Too many people were here yesterday."

Frustrated, he thanked the man, then went back outside. He sat on one of the painted benches under a tree and stared across the grounds to the broken tracks. Someone had done it deliberately. They had known that that part of the track wasn't monitored. They had known that they wouldn't be caught.

An insider, he thought. *Someone who could walk across it without being suspect. Someone who had inside information about the security setup.*

He rushed back into the office building and hurried down the hall to the personnel office. No one was there today. Andi had given the office staff the day off, for she'd been too despondent to think of any work that could be done when she didn't even plan to open the park now. He went to the file cabinets lining the walls and found the one marked, "Engineers." He flipped through, until he found all of those who worked on the FanTran. One by one, he slipped them out into a sloppy stack on the floor. Then he went to the cabinet marked, "Security." All of those assigned to that area of the park were added to the stack. He moved to the "Maintenance" drawer, and did the same.

By the time he'd pulled the file of everyone who'd had anything to do with the FanTran, he had a stack at least a yard tall. He sat down on the floor and began to read through the files for anything that might clue him. There was quite possibly someone within this stack who had a background or a former job or a skill or an association that might clue him. Anything. There had to be.

You've got to help me, Lord. Don't let them win.

He began to go through each file, reading every word. Night fell, and grew old, and then dawn came, before he'd gone through all of them.

By morning, he had five employees that he considered suspects. One had a two-year inexplicable unemployment on his resumé, something that often indicated that he either had a job he didn't want to report for whatever reason, had been in jail, had been ill, or had encountered an incredible run of bad fortune. He doubted it was the latter, but intended to find out which of the others explained it.

Another had once been employed by one of the businesses that Givens owned. In fact, he'd held a position much higher than he held here. That, he thought, was a little suspicious.

The other three files had inconsistencies regarding overlapping dates of employments, educational backgrounds, etc., things that could have been typographical errors. But Justin intended to take no chances.

Bone-tired, he made a call to Henry Baxter, a retired police officer and one of his father's former partners.

The man's raspy voice reminded Justin of the early hour. He'd awakened him.

"Y-ello."

"Henry? This is Justin Pierce. Robert's boy?"

"Justin!" the man said. "Well, I'll be. Sure didn't expect to hear from you so early in the morning."

"I'm sorry I woke you, Henry. But it's an emergency. I need for you to pull some strings at the police station to get me some information. Do you still have any clout there?"

"I should. I was on the force for forty-two years. What do you need?"

"I'm working for Promised Land, Henry. You probably heard about the accident here."

"Yeah. Good thing no one was killed."

"Sure is. The thing is, I think it was sabotage, maybe an inside job, and I've narrowed it down to five employees who might have something to do with it. I need any information you can get me on them."

"I can do that," he said. "Tell you what. Give me an hour to get down to the station, and meet me there with whatever you already have. It shouldn't be a problem. I still know everybody there. Used to be boss to most of them."

"I knew you could do it, Henry. I'll see you in an hour."

He met his father's old friend at the station, and was startled by how much the man had aged. But he still seemed to command a great deal of respect at the police station. They quickly gave him a desk at which to work, and he began to peck information into the computer that would call up rap sheets, credit reports, phone records, and other information on the men Justin suspected.

When all the information had been printed out, he slipped the old man a hundred dollar bill and thanked him profusely. Henry, who seemed to miss his police work, asked him to let him know if there was anything else he could do. Justin promised him he would.

Activity was just resuming around the accident scene as Justin made it back to the park. It didn't occur to him that he hadn't showered since yesterday or that he was wearing these clothes for the second day in a row. He was too anxious to study the information he'd compiled on these men. He went up to his office, locked himself in, and studied the records more intently than he'd ever studied anything in his life.

One by one, he eliminated men, as explanations became apparent and inconsistencies were cleared up. Finally, he was down to one man. The one who had worked for one of Givens's companies—a man named Allen Jenkins.

He pulled out the phone record and studied the numbers. They meant nothing to him unless he had the names that went with them. Frustrated, he called Henry back. "I'm sorry to bother you again, Henry, but do you have any way of getting the names that go with these phone numbers?"

"Give me a few minutes," Henry said. "I'll get back to you."

A few minutes later, the phone rang, and Justin snatched it up. It was Henry on a three-way call with a friend of his from the phone company. "This call never happened, Justin. But tell my friend here the numbers you're interested in, and he'll tell you who they belong to."

Justin began reading the numbers off, and the unidentified voice gave him the names. The moment he got to Givens's name, he knew he'd hit pay dirt. There were at least fifteen calls to or from Givens to this particular security guard in the last three weeks. Funny thing, since the man had allegedly been fired from his job with one of Givens's companies.

He tried to think clearly, in spite of his fatigue. If Givens was behind this, was he behind the arson, too? He closed his eyes, rubbed them roughly, then had an idea. "I need one more thing, guys. I need the phone record of a man named Charles Butler. Can you get that for me?"

"How about it?" Henry asked his friend.

"Sure," the man said. "What's your fax number?"

He gave it to him, and in seconds, the printout was coming through his machine. He jerked it out before the machine could cut it, and searched for Givens's number. There it was—at least a dozen times in the two weeks prior to the arson.

"Thank you so much, both of you," he said. "If this works out, you'll both get lifelong tickets to Promised Land."

He hung up and raced to the elevator, got off on Andi and Wes's floor, and ran to Andi's office. She wasn't there. He turned and hurried down to Wes's, and found them both sitting wearily at his conference table. "I've figured it out!" he said, bursting into the room. "Givens is behind it. Charles Butler—the arsonist—was working for him, and so is one of our security guards. I've got their phone records, and they were both in touch with him over a dozen times each right before the sabotage."

Andi stood up, stricken, and Wes followed. "Justin, are you sure?" Wes asked. "Can you prove this?"

"Not yet," he said. "Not quite. But Charlie Butler is already in jail, and we can get a confession out of him. Givens is letting him take the fall, and by now, I'll bet he's busting to get even. The other guy will spill his guts, too, as soon as I get my hands around his throat. I thought you two might want to come be witnesses to this grand event."

He turned and headed back to the elevators.

"Justin!" he heard Andi shout as the doors closed behind him. But he didn't intend to be stopped until he'd gotten the truth out where everyone could see it.

Justin's first stop was to the security house, where he found Allen Jenkins, the man in question, and feigning friendship and respect, asked him to come help him with something. Putting his arm around him, he escorted him to the accident scene, where two inspectors were videotaping and photographing the scene. The parish engineer who had ordered him off of the track yesterday looked up at him as he approached with the guard, and Andi and Wes were fast approaching from across the grounds.

When Justin turned to face the engineer, his arm still thrown across the shoulders of the guard, the man's steps faltered.

"I want to know something," said Justin. "Who did this investigation and filled out the initial report on the crash?"

The man cleared his voice and glanced around him. "Well . . . I did."

"Then tell me," Justin bit out in a murderously quiet voice, as he took slow, menacing steps toward him, still holding onto the guard. "Are you blind . . . or are you in B.W. Givens's pocket, too?"

Allen Jenkins stiffened beneath Justin's arm, and the inspector began to fidget. The group of men beside the building ceased their conversations. "I . . . I don't know what you—"

Justin pointed to the rails over his head. "I'm talking about the fact that the spikes were removed on about twenty feet of rail. I'm talking about the missing joint bar. I'm talking about a cover-up!"

The inspector began to step backward, but Justin's hands shot out and took him by the collar, jerking him upward until the short man's face was closer to the frightening eyes that bored into him. "Why did you cover up? Did you have something to do with the sabotage?"

"What . . . I . . . No . . ." the man stammered.

Fury seethed through Justin's veins, and he was on the verge of explosion. "Funny thing is, Givens isn't going to cover for you. Remember the fire that was started a few weeks ago? He's still letting Charlie Butler take the heat. Poor man's sitting in jail, waiting for trial or for big, important Givens to bail him out, but he's not going to. And he won't bail you out, either. He'd as soon throw you to the wolves as remember your name."

Allen Jenkins started to walk away, so Justin released the inspector and grabbed the security guard. Holding his collar in both fists, he dragged the guard close to his face. "And you . . . protecting the park from the forces of evil . . . who woulda thought that you might be one of Givens's puppets, that you might have known what part of the tracks weren't covered by cameras, and that you might have gotten up there without being noticed and pulled those bolts? Who would have believed it?"

"Hey, man. I didn't do anything like that . . . I would never do anything to hurt Promised Land!"

"We have phone records, pal. We have your bank deposits. And you didn't really think that Givens was going to get you out of this, did you? Give you an alibi? Bail you out? No. In fact, he has some interesting stories to tell about you." It was a bluff, and he didn't know for sure if it would work. But he was the king of the bluffers.

Andi seethed with rage. "We've been led to believe that you were the mastermind," she said, adding to the bluff. "That you may have planned the whole thing."

"That sleazeball told you that?" the engineer cried. "He told you that *I* masterminded it? Let me tell you something! If it weren't for me, it might have happened when people were around it. I'm the one who made sure that no one got hurt! If it weren't for me, it would have wound up like the fire, almost killing someone. Or the car wreck ..." He caught himself and cursed, then kicked at the ground.

Andi and Justin exchanged glances, and there was a collective gasp from all of those around them. Then dead, barren silence.

"What car wreck?" Andi asked.

He clammed up, unwilling to say another word.

"What car wreck?" she shouted. "My father's? Was Givens behind my father's wreck?"

The guard was shaking now, and he muttered, "I'm not saying another word until I have a lawyer."

Andi, too, was shaking, and her eyes filled with tears. "We can make a deal with you. If you talk, and tell us everything you know that Givens has done, and testify against him when we get him to trial, I can guarantee you that we'll drop all charges against you. Both of you. But if you don't, I can promise you that you'll rot in jail along with him, if it takes every last ounce of energy I have to make it happen."

"Get me a lawyer, and I'll tell you everything I know," the engineer said.

The guard was almost in tears as he nodded his head. "Get me one, too," he said. "And I'll talk."

They had the guards they trusted take them away until their lawyers could get there, and Andi stood frozen for a long moment, staring after them as the reality of what had happened sank into her. "Givens was responsible for my father's death," she said. "He caused the accident. He killed him . . ."

Justin didn't care that she had sent him away, called him deadweight, told him she didn't love him. He slid his arms around her and held her, only caring that she had some comfort from the ugly realities she had encountered today.

"Just hold me for a minute," she whispered. "Don't let me go."

"You should know by now," he whispered, his trembling arms crushing her more desperately against him, "that I have no intentions of ever doing that again."

Chapter Twenty-Seven

Because of the mountain of evidence that came in like an avalanche regarding Givens's part in the crimes against Promised Land, and the eyewitness accounts from people who were either approached about doing mischief on the grounds or hired to do it, not to mention the fact that the security guard swore to the fact that Givens had been responsible for Andrew Sherman's accident, the man decided to plead guilty to extortion, conspiracy, slander, and manslaughter—a charge that had been bargained down in order to get his confession.

Three months later, he was sentenced to thirty-five years in prison—not enough for Andi, but enough to get him out of her way as she finished Promised Land. He was also ordered to pay her significant damages, an amount even higher than her insurance had already paid.

One morning, as she and Justin stood in the tower overlooking the park, where they had stood together on that first day that they'd signed the papers making Justin a part of Promised Land, she felt more peace than she'd felt in months. The Hands Across the Sea area had been rebuilt in record time, and the FanTran was finished, as well. Her investors had come to her aid to finance the rebuilding, knowing full well that the park would more than earn it back as soon as it opened.

"I can't believe it's almost finished," she whispered as the breeze whipped through her hair. "Can you?"

"Yeah," he said. "I can. There it is."

She smiled. "What would I have done without you, Justin? I'd be bankrupt. I'd be cowering in a corner somewhere, and Givens would have won."

"You cowering? I don't think so."

"I don't know," she said. "I've cowered from you an awful lot. God sure has taught me some lessons, Justin."

He turned his back to the rail and leaned against it, gazing at her. "What lessons?"

"About my pride. About real repentance. About how self-defeating it is to always win."

"Yeah," he said. "Sometimes you need to lose, don't you? Just to keep you humble." He slid his hands into his pockets. "I can relate. God's had to bend me and break me and chip away at me to make me more like him. I still have an awful long way to go."

"But look at his provision. He brought us together, with all our flaws, and knew that we would help lift each other up. Amazing, isn't it?"

"Not so amazing when you consider that it was all a part of his plan. To bring us together. To see us get married."

Her eyes shot up to his, and he caught her chin and held it so she wouldn't break his gaze. "Andi, it's time."

"Time for what?" she asked with a coy smile.

"Time to marry me," he said. "The park's opening next month. I think that's ample time to plan a wedding."

Her eyes widened. "You want to get married before the park opens?"

"Nope," he said. "*When* the park opens. I want to get married on opening day, just like we planned."

She stared at him for a moment as tears filled her eyes, then finally reached up to slide her arms around his neck. "I think that's a beautiful idea, Justin."

"Really?" he asked. "Even though it was mine?"

"*Because* it was yours," she said.

A month later, Andi stood beside Justin, her gown shimmering in the white-gold sunlight. Justin smiled down at her, running his finger around the inside edge of his stiff collar as if he couldn't wait to be rid of it.

The minister stepped to the bell tower railing of Khaki's Kastle, and smiled down on the thousands of people below them who had packed into the Promised Land grounds for opening day and the fairy-tale wedding. With a triumphant smile, the minister spread his arms wide. "I now pronounce you man and wife," he shouted dramatically as the crowd roared in wild excitement. Hundreds of colorful balloons rose to sprinkle the sky, and streamers and confetti floated everywhere.

"Shall I kiss the bride?" Justin inquired with an insufferable grin as he pulled Andi into his arms.

"If you don't, I'm pushing you over," Andi teased, sliding her arms around his neck and letting the forgotten bouquet hang from her fingertips as he dipped and kissed her.

His kiss was drugging, exhilarating, promising, awakening desire that would have to wait. A cheer rose from the crowd, then a unanimous demand for the bouquet. Justin broke the kiss and looked around, distracted. "Uh . . . I think they want the bouquet."

She laughed and looked over the rail to the friends, family, and patrons below them. "Where should I toss it?"

Justin looked out over her shoulder until he found Sherry standing beside Madeline. "How about over there?" he asked. "It might cheer Sherry up."

Taking aim, Andi leaned forward and launched the bouquet. Madeline dove for it, but it fell into Sherry's hands. She looked stunned for a moment, then forced a smile and waved up at them. "I hope Clint comes back," Justin said. "I think Sherry deserves to be as happy as we are."

The Promised Land band struck up, and all of Khaki's Krewe began to dance hilariously. "We really did it," Andi said, turning back to Justin.

"God did it," Justin whispered. "In spite of us." Justin turned her to face him and pulled her into his arms. "I think we have a few hours until the reception," he whispered against her ear, referring to the Downtown, Planet Earth party they had scheduled for that night, the party that would remain a nightly Promised Land event. "Why don't we try to slip away?"

"You're on," she said. "Let's go."

He reached down and swept her up in his arms and carried her down the long staircase to the coach that awaited them.

Wes and Laney, with Amy and the baby, leaned into the chariot before it moved. Wes pressed a kiss on her cheek, then clutched Justin's hand in silent blessing. He stepped back, and Andi's mother—looking tanned and radiant from her stint in Paris—embraced them both joyfully. "In all the world, I couldn't have picked a better husband for my daughter," she told Justin. "Her father would be so proud."

Smiling, Justin kissed her cheek. She stepped back, and the joyous crowd parted as the white steeds marched through, pulling the coach that carried the lovers.

Khaki, Ned, Trudeau, and all the rest of the Krewe gave mock salutes to their animator on their right, and on the left Andi's uniformed park employees waved joyously. But Andi and Justin were oblivious to the cheers and congratulations over their married dreams, for they were lost in a new one that took them far beyond today. A dream that God had ordained.

And in that dream they were both winners.

About the Author

Terri Blackstock is an award-winning novelist who has written for several major publishers including HarperCollins, Dell, Harlequin, and Silhouette. Published under two pseudonyms, her books have sold over 5 million copies worldwide.

With her success in secular publishing at its peak, Blackstock had what she calls "a spiritual awakening." A Christian since the age of fourteen, she realized she had not been using her gift as God intended. It was at that point that she recommitted her life to Christ, gave up her secular career, and made the decision to write only books that would point her readers to him.

"I wanted to be able to tell the truth in my stories," she said, "and not just be politically correct. It doesn't matter how many readers I have if I can't tell them what I know about the roots of their problems and the solutions that have literally saved my own life."

Her books are about flawed Christians in crisis and God's provisions for their mistakes and wrong choices. She claims to be extremely qualified to write such books, since she's had years of personal experience.

A native of nowhere, since she was raised in the Air Force, Blackstock makes Mississippi her home. She and her husband are the parents of three children—a blended family which she considers one more of God's provisions.

Enjoy the next book in the Second Chances Series

Blind Trust

Chapter 1

The Bronco that had been riding Sherry Grayson's bumper since she'd left work was not the sole cause of her rising anger. But since it had been inappropriate to lash out at Madeline when she'd broken the news just fifteen minutes ago, she figured the Bronco was as good a target for her rancor as any.

Deliberately slowing to fifteen miles an hour in a forty-mile-an-hour zone, she crept along, hoping the driver behind her would get the message and pass her before she gave in to her instincts and slammed her brakes to make him hit her from behind. It would serve him right, she thought. But wrecking her car wouldn't solve her problems, any more than bursting into tears would. And she had neither the time nor the energy for that.

"Slow down," she muttered as tremors of anxiety coursed through her. She couldn't deal with a battle with a joyrider today. Yesterday, when life still had as much normalcy as it had had for the last eight months, she might have handled it better. But today . . .

"Get off my bumper!" Sherry blared, heat scoring her features when the Bronco almost bumped her. Heavy traffic detoured around them, but the driver would not pass her. It was an omen, she thought, an omen that her refusal to look back wouldn't do the trick anymore. After what she'd learned today, she knew she'd have to look back to muster the strength to plunge forward into the inevitable.

According to her roommate, Clint Jessup was back from the black hole he'd vanished into without a trace eight months ago, and he intended to see her. The destructive driver behind her was a warning that life was going to be a bit rougher for a while. But she had braved rough times before, and she had no doubt she could do it again.

Dreadfully anxious to be rid of the vehicle that seemed bent on driving right through her, she made a sharp turn onto a quieter street and breathed a shaky sigh of relief that she could drive the rest of the way in peace.

But a quick glance in the rearview mirror told her the Bronco was still behind her. Her pulse accelerated as the first light of understanding dawned on her. The Bronco was following her.

Driving fast enough to keep a car's distance between them, Sherry strained to make out the driver. A man—no, two men—sat silhouetted against the sun descending at their backs. The driver's shoulders were squared with determination as he drove, and the passenger sat slumped against the door in a pose of utter boredom. An instant of panic surged through her, and her chest constricted with air that couldn't find its way out.

Making another quick turn while she held her breath, Sherry watched in her mirror as the Bronco barreled around the corner after her, the sun no longer making opaque shadows out of her pursuers. The driver's hair flapped into his face from the hard wind at his window, and she watched a hand come up to push it back into place. It was dark hair, full and tapering back from his face, and against the light through his back window she could see the slightest hint of curl.

She made another turn as the panic coiling in the pit of her stomach became more pronounced. The sun was blazing toward her now, and without slowing her speed, she held up a hand to shade her eyes and glanced in the mirror again, hoping to glimpse his features and report him to the police. Sherry clutched the steering wheel more tightly as she waited for the bright glare to slide off the windshield and give her a clear view of his face as they rounded a curve. The open collar of the driver's shirt flapped against his neck and a ray of sunlight caught a strip of gold draping down from his throat, illuminating it like the razor edge of a knife aimed at her. Some familiar pain stabbed her heart and she released her breath in a rush. *The gold chain . . . the engagement gift she had given him . . .*

"No," she said aloud before her imagination carried her away. It wasn't him. It was just the knowledge that he was back that had made her heart conjure up images.

The sun descended behind the trees after its last blinding burst of orange, and suddenly the man came into full view through the mirror—the beckoning mane of soft, dark hair, the determined set of full lips on a tanned face, the chain glistening more subtly against his neck. And as her punctured heart sank to her stomach, her eyes rose to the dark, riveting eyes that refused to let her go.

Clint Jessup's eyes.

Oh, dear God, I'm not ready for this. Physical danger she could bear, but Clint Jessup threatened something far worse.

Suddenly her driving became uninhibited, and her foot slammed against the accelerator. The sound and feel of metal sent a chill through her bones to rival the heat of the rage still consuming her.

As if he knew he'd been recognized, Clint's teeth flashed between tight lips, and he sped up as well. His shoulders hunched forward as he clutched the steering wheel. Searching for another turnoff in hopes of getting back into the flow and security of heavy traffic, Sherry forced her eyes to stay on the road and away from the rearview mirror. But no sooner had she spotted a turnoff a mile up the deserted road than the heavy hum of his engine loomed up beside her.

Sherry kept her eyes off the vehicle trying to stop her, and remained intent on reaching the turnoff. But Clint had other plans. She heard his gears shift, heard the passenger in his car shouting at him, heard the squeal of his tires as he found a last burst of speed and screeched sideways in front of her. Stomping on her brakes, she steered to the shoulder of the road, skidding to a stop just short of hitting him.

The driver's door of the Bronco slammed, and in seconds Clint was at her car. Before the thought of locking her door occurred to her, he was reaching for the handle, opening it, leaning inside. Sherry shoved him away and pushed out of the car, her lungs groping for air, her heart pounding. "Have you become a lunatic as well as a coward? Are you trying to kill us?"

Clint leaned against her car door to close it. The suggestion of a smile softened his lips, but his black eyes were serious as they took in the sight of her. "Hi, Sherry," he said.

The mildness of his greeting rankled her, but somehow she couldn't make herself get back in the car and drive away just yet. "What do you want, Clint?"

"I just wanted to see you. I tried to call, but I didn't get very far with your roommate."

Sherry slid her trembling fists into the pockets of her pants. "In the old days they used to knock on doors for that sort of thing, instead of running you down in the street."

"You would have just slammed the door in my face," Clint said. "I wanted to catch you before you got inside."

Sherry turned away from his probing eyes and peered up the street, wishing she could turn back time a half hour and prepare herself for this encounter. "Next time you want to follow someone, Superman, you might be less conspicuous if you kept a few inches between bumpers."

A slow, half-smile sauntered across Clint's face, casting an angular shadow on the new, deep lines in his bronze skin. "And next time you get followed, Lois, you might avoid taking the most deserted street in the city."

Sherry shrugged and reached past his hip to open her door. "Lesson learned. Now, if you'll excuse me."

Clint caught her shoulders and turned her to face him, his eyes narrow slashes squinting down at her. "I wanted to see you, Sherry, not teach you a lesson."

Sherry stepped out of his hold and assessed him guardedly, fighting back the hope that told her to give him a chance. Reason left her for a fleeting moment, her eyes softened, and she mentally brushed his hair back as it eased over his face, mentally straightened the long, thin strand of gold as it looped from his neck where she had hung it months ago, mentally traced the tapering lines of his white shirt, the jeans that were worn and faded, the threadbare jogging shoes that he had never been able to part with as easily as he'd parted with her.

"Why did you move?" he asked. "I thought I'd never find you."

Sherry glanced away long enough to tighten her tenuous grip on her unstable emotions, then brought her eyes back to his, unblinking, as if the simple movement would shatter them. "I was all packed up with no place to go."

His doleful gaze lowered to the pavement between them, and his throat convulsed. "I know I hurt you, running out like that before the wedding, but—"

"I survived," she cut in, desperately wanting to be spared the excuses that had taken him eight months to manufacture. She already knew the reason he had left. When Madeline had called her this afternoon to tell her that Clint was back and that he had called, she'd said something about his being away working on a book he was writing. The very idea had enraged Sherry. He wasn't a writer. He had never even mentioned a desire to write. He had been a youth minister before he'd skipped town. The flimsy, stupid excuse for his fleeing from commitment had added insult to injury.

"It was great to see you again, Clint," she said in a saccharine voice as she reached for her door again. "Next time you see me on the street feel free to run me off the road for a nice little chat." The door snapped open beneath her hand, but before she could step inside, Clint's fingers clamped like iron cuffs around her arm.

Though his pressure would have swung her to face him, she deliberately kept her body turned toward the car. "I'm not finished with you, Sherry," he said in a firm, determined voice as he set his other hand on her stiffening shoulder.

The touch shattered her facade and exposed the raw pain hidden beneath it. She clamped her teeth shut, grating out words that cut deeper with each syllable. "What do you want?"

"I want you back," he said simply.

An almost hysterical laugh came from deep in her throat. Slowly, she turned to face him, carefully disengaging her arm from his grasp and narrowing her blue eyes to hide the pain lurking there. "It's about eight months too late for that, Clint. I must admit, I didn't expect you to work the freedom bug out of your system quite so soon, but—"

"It wasn't the freedom bug, Sherry," Clint interrupted impatiently. "You can't believe I would have skipped out on the wedding without a really good reason."

Sherry shook her head wearily and gazed off into the distance, the well of moisture in her eyes catching the light. "Clint, how should I put this? If you were kidnapped by savages and taken to some exotic island, and had to spend eight months swimming shark-infested waters to get back to me, it wouldn't make any difference. It's over. Dead. Can you understand that?"

His throat bobbed again, and he raised a finger to her chin, coaxing her face back to his in such a gentle way that she couldn't resist looking at him. "I don't believe you."

Swallowing back the emotion blocking her throat, Sherry steadied her voice. "Fine, then, let's test it. *Were* you kidnapped by savages and taken to some exotic island . . . ?" As she spoke, full tears sprang to her eyes, for she hadn't realized until now how much she wished it were true.

"No," he said. A deep, jagged breath tore from his lungs. "I can't make you understand right now. I had to get away and—"

"Write?" The word was flung as a challenge.

The lines in Clint's face seemed etched deep with regret as he looked at the ground, then glanced toward the quiet man still sitting in the Bronco, the man Sherry had almost forgotten. The man leaned forward and nodded, as if giving him some silent signal. Clint's eyes glossed over with despair as he brought them back to her. "Yeah," he breathed out in a voice as dull as the sky in the wake of sunset. "I had to get away and write."

Somehow the admission pierced her even more deeply than his disappearance had. "I'm sure the youth ministers of the world will appreciate the sacrifices you've made to record your amazing wellspring of knowledge. Too bad you've lost all your credibility now that you've left your youth group high and dry and dumped your fiancé all in one moment of panic."

"Sherry, don't do this," he whispered. He touched her hair so lightly that she sensed more than felt it. "I've been through agony, and it's not over yet."

Sherry ducked her head away from his hand and slipped into the car. "Just think how much richer your writing will be after all that suffering," she said, her voice cracking. She cranked her engine, but he leaned inside the car door, still not letting her go.

"It's not over, Sherry," he said in a deep, desperate voice. "I'm not giving up on you. You're gonna have to do one major convincing job to make me believe that you don't care anymore."

Sherry stared at her trembling hands clutching the steering wheel as if it alone could anchor her to reality.

"I'm still crazy about you," he whispered, his hand slipping through the dark fall of her hair to settle on her neck. "An hour hasn't gone by that I haven't thought of you."

Sherry knew that somewhere within her there must be some reserve of strength. But for the life of her, she could not find it. Her eyes fluttered shut, absorbing the welling beads of moisture. She opened them again as his fingers began to knead her neck. "That's very touching," she whispered without inflection. Moving her head forward, she reached for his wrist and shoved his hand away from her neck. "Now if you'll kindly move so I can shut my door . . ."

"I want to see you tonight."

"No."

"Why not?" he asked. "What are you afraid of?"

"My temper," she said.

"I know that temper. I can deal with it."

"I can't," she bit out, lips quivering. "It might land me in jail." Her face reddened to back up the words, seething blood and storming emotions threatening to implode, leaving her their only victim, if she didn't start driving.

"Then when can I see you?" The question was a pleading whisper against her face.

"Never. Now get away from my car."

Clint opened his mouth to speak again, but only a frustrated breath escaped. "I'll let you go now, but it's not over by a long shot."

Sherry slipped her car into reverse. "It's your time, your energy. Waste it if you want."

Slowly, Clint stepped back and allowed her to pull her door closed. He stood watching as she backed away from the Bronco's barricade, then shifted into drive with a screech of rubber and went around it.

Numbness was something Sherry would have sold her soul for at that moment, for her heart ached enormously as she glanced back at him before making her turn. He was leaning against the Bronco as he stared after her. Quickly, she turned, leaving him behind, though the sight of him was inexorably drafted on her mind.

(ISBN #: 0-310-20710-X)

GRAND RAPIDS, MICHIGAN 49530 USA

WWW.ZONDERVAN.COM

Last Light

Terri Blackstock

Today, the world as you know it will end.
No need to turn off the lights.

Your car suddenly stalls and won't restart.
You can't call for help because your cell phone is dead.
Everyone around you is having the same problem ...
and it's just the tip of the iceberg.

Your city is in a blackout. Communication is cut off.
Hospital equipment won't operate.
And airplanes are falling from the sky.

Is it a terrorist attack ... or something far worse?

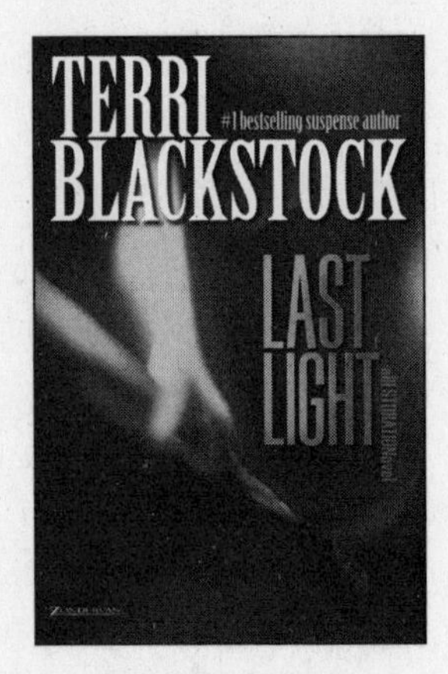

In the face of a crisis that sweeps an entire high-tech planet back to the age before electricity, Deni Branning's career ambitions have vanished. She's not about to let her dream of marriage go as well.

But keeping it alive will require extraordinary measures. Yesterday's world is gone. All Deni and her family have left is each other and their neighbors. Their little community will either stand or fall together. But they're only beginning to realize it—and trust doesn't come easily.

Particularly when one of them is a killer.

Bestselling suspense author Terri Blackstock weaves a masterful what-if novel in which global catastrophe reveals the darkness in human hearts—and lights the way to restoration for a self-centered world.

Softcover: 0-310-25767-0

Emerald Windows

Terri Blackstock, #1 Bestselling Suspense Author

Ten years ago, devastated by an ugly scandal, Brooke Martin fled the small town of Hayden to pursue a career as a stained glass artist. Now Brooke has returned on business to discover that some things never change. Her spotted reputation remains. Tongues still wag. And that makes what should be her dream assignment tough.

Brooke has been hired to design new stained glass windows at Hayden Bible Church. The job is a career windfall. But Nick Marcello is overseeing the project, and some in the church think Nick and Brooke's relationship is not entirely professional—and as before, there is no convincing those people otherwise.

In the face of mounting rumors, the two set out to produce the masterpiece Nick has conceived: a brilliant set of windows displaying God's covenants in the Bible. For Brooke, it is more than a project—it is a journey toward faith. But opposition is heating up. A vicious battle of words and will is about to tax Brooke's commitment to the limit. Only this time, she is determined not to run.

Softcover 0-310-22807-7

Pick up a copy today at your favorite bookstore!

Cape Refuge Series

This bestselling series follows the lives of the people of the small seaside community of Cape Refuge, as two sisters struggle to continue the ministry their parents began helping the troubled souls who come to Hanover House for solace.

Cape Refuge
Softcover: 0-310-23592-8

Southern Storm
Softcover: 0-310-23593-6

River's Edge
Softcover: 0-310-23594-4

Breaker's Reef
Softcover: 0-310-23595-2

ZONDERVAN®
GRAND RAPIDS, MICHIGAN 49530 USA
WWW.ZONDERVAN.COM

Other favorites from Terri Blackstock . . .

Newpointe 911 Series

Softcover 0-310-21757-1

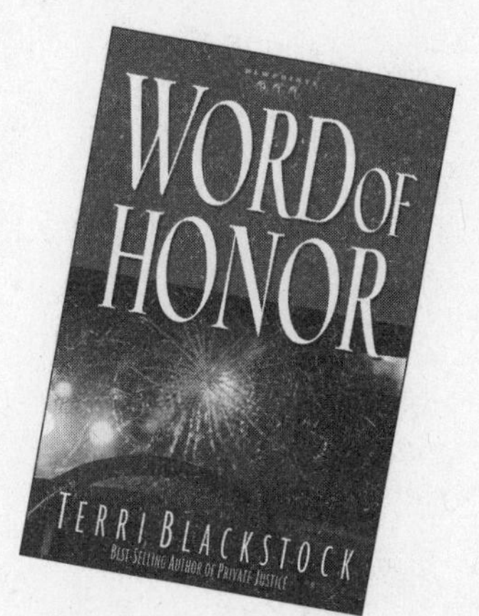

Softcover 0-310-21759-8

Softcover 0-310-21758-X

Softcover 0-310-21760-1

Softcover 0-310-25064-1

Pick up a copy today at your favorite bookstore!

GRAND RAPIDS, MICHIGAN 49530 USA

WWW.ZONDERVAN.COM

Seaside

Terri Blackstock

Seaside is a novella of the heart—poignant, gentle, true, offering an eloquent reminder that life is too precious a gift to be unwrapped in haste.

Sarah Rivers has it all: successful husband, healthy kids, beautiful home, meaningful church work.

Corinne, Sarah's sister, struggles to get by. From Web site development to jewelry sales, none of the pies she has her thumb stuck in contains a plum worth pulling.

No wonder Corinne envies Sarah. What she doesn't know is how jealous Sarah is of her. And what neither of them realizes is how their frantic drive for achievement is speeding them headlong past the things that matter most in life.

So when their mother, Maggie, purchases plane tickets for them to join her in a vacation on the Gulf of Mexico, they almost decline the offer. But circumstances force the issue, and the sisters soon find themselves first thrown together, then ultimately *drawn* together, in one memorable week in a cabin called "Seaside."

As Maggie, a professional photographer, sets out to capture on film the faces and moods of her daughters, more than film develops. A picture emerges of possibilities that come only by slowing down and savoring the simple treasures of the moment. It takes a mother's love and honesty to teach her two daughters a wiser, uncluttered way of life—one that can bring peace to their hearts and healing to their relationship. And though the lesson comes on wings of grief, the sadness is tempered with faith, restoration, and a joy that comes from the hand of God.

Hardcover: 0-310-23318-6

Pick up a copy today at your favorite bookstore!

GRAND RAPIDS, MICHIGAN 49530 USA

WWW.ZONDERVAN.COM

Three ways to keep up on your favorite Zondervan books and authors

Sign up for our *Fiction E-Newsletter*. Every month you'll receive sample excerpts from our books, sneak peeks at upcoming books, and chances to win free books autographed by the author.

You can also sign up for our *Breakfast Club*. Every morning in your email, you'll receive a five-minute snippet from a fiction or nonfiction book. A new book will be featured each week, and by the end of the week you will have sampled two to three chapters of the book.

Zondervan *Author Tracker* is the best way to be notified whenever your favorite Zondervan authors write new books, go on tour, or want to tell you about what's happening in their lives.

Visit *www.zondervan.com* and sign up today!